No Escape

MEREDITH FLETCHER

First published in Great Britain 2013
by Mills & Boon, an imprint of Harlequin (UK) Limited.
Large Print edition 2013
Harlequin (UK) Limited,
Eton House, 18-24 Paradise Road,
Richmond, Surrey TW9 1SR

© Meredith Fletcher 2012

ISBN: 978 0 263 23805 1

Printed and bound in Great Britain
by CPI Antony Rowe, Chippenham, Wiltshire

"I know magic."

"Sure you do."

He studied her with indolent eyes, not saying anything until she recited his address.

His defenses went up. "How do you know so much about me?"

"Like I said, magic." Lauren raised her right hand, palm forward so he couldn't see the driver's license trapped by its edge between her first two fingers.

"I'm not a big believer in magic."

With a flourish, Lauren shook her hand and his driver's license appeared at the end of her fingers. For a moment, Heath didn't know what to say. Before he could recover, she flicked her wrist and sent the plastic rectangle spinning at him.

Heath caught the license in his left hand. His free hand slid down to his pants pocket, then he looked surprised. "You picked my pocket at the morgue."

MEREDITH FLETCHER

lives out West where the skies are big, but still close enough to Los Angeles to slip in for some strategic shopping. She loves old stores with real wooden floors, open-air cafés, comfortable boots, the mountains and old movies like *Portrait of Jennie* while sipping a cup of hot cocoa on a frosty day. She's previously written for Silhouette Bombshell and loves action romances with larger-than-life heroes and heroines with pithy repartee. She has pithy repartee herself, but never when she seems to need it most! She's much more comfortable at the computer writing her books. Please contact her at meredithfletcher@hotmail.com or find her at www.whatmakesmyheartbeatfaster.blogspot.com

For Matt and Alyssa,
who found each other.

Chapter 1

"I'm sorry about your friend."

Throttling the urge to scream in rage and pain, Lauren Cooper stared down at the body of Megan Taylor. "She's— She wasn't my friend. We were sisters."

On the other side of the stainless-steel table that supported Megan, the coroner consulted a small spiral-bound notebook. Intensity clung to him like a second skin. He didn't look like a guy who smiled much, but he was handsome and would have had a nice smile when he put himself to it.

Being a coroner wasn't a profession that lent itself to a lot of smiles, though. Not even in Jamaica.

His white lab coat was stretched tight across broad shoulders. The notebook nearly disappeared in his big, callused hands. A faded half-moon scar showed on the left side of his cleft chin. He was over thirty, but not by much. He was six feet plus and lean. His sun-streaked bronze hair was short and neat, professional, but a little long now, a little out of control. Maybe he hit the beach a lot when he wasn't in the morgue. His accent was Southern, somewhere in the lower forty-eight.

Lauren turned her attention from the coroner and focused on Megan. Looking at her lying there on the table was the hardest thing Lauren had ever had to do. Mornings filled with pillow fights, nights packed with shared secrets, all the things sisters did made the reality even more confusing.

Megan's short-cropped platinum-blond hair was tangled with seaweed, and Lauren knew that she would never have wanted to be seen like that. She had to resist the impulse to comb the debris from Megan's hair.

You can't. It's evidence. It's all evidence. Tears burned the backs of Lauren's eyes.

Megan is evidence now.

The thought almost wrung a howl of pain from Lauren. She curled her hands into fists and made herself breathe, made herself push the air out and slowly let it back in. She had to keep the air going out. It was too easy to hold it in.

Looking at Megan's body lying on the table and covered to the neck by the white sheet was a nightmare. She'd been twenty-seven years old, the same age Lauren was. Both of them were similarly built, athletic with curves.

With her fair hair and dazzling blue eyes, Megan had been the one of them that was the light. Dark haired and dark eyed, Lauren had been the shadow. Megan had always fearlessly rushed in, and Lauren had always waited on the outside, watching before she dove in.

That had changed later. Megan had remained fearless, but Lauren had learned to seize the limelight whenever she needed to. Success in her job had depended on that. She was suddenly aware of the silence in the morgue, and that the coroner was staring at her.

She thought back frantically, trying to remember any question she might have missed.

There were so many questions swirling through her head right now. "I'm sorry. Did you ask me something?"

"I did. Which of you is married?"

The question surprised Lauren. It didn't seem like the kind of information a coroner would want. But this was Jamaica. She didn't know how things worked down here. She'd never been to the island country.

"Neither of us is married."

The coroner's eyes were gold with green flakes that stirred restlessly. He didn't blink. "Different last names. Is one of you divorced?"

"No."

"But you said you're sisters?"

"Yes. I was adopted." *Rescued* was more like it. Lauren still had nightmares about the orphanage and foster homes. Her adoptive mother told her those memories would fade, but they hadn't. Lauren had always been thankful for the second chance she'd gotten, and being orphaned once had made losing her adoptive father to a heart attack four years ago even harder. Megan and her mother were all that Lauren had left.

And now Megan was gone.

"You kept your birth name?"

"Yes. It was all I had left of my parents." Lauren had wanted to keep something from them. They had died tragically. It hadn't been their fault that they'd left her. From everything she remembered of them, they had been good people.

"Do you know who Ms. Taylor came down here with?"

"She came by herself." Lauren looked down at her sister. There had been so many wild things Megan had gotten her to do when they'd lived at home and during college.

"Was she in the habit of doing things like that?"

Lauren kept her voice soft. "She liked her adventures."

"Adventures?"

"That's what she called them. Her adventures." Lauren's eyes burned, but she refused to let the tears fall. She wasn't going to do that in front this stranger. She had always been emotionally reserved.

Except with Megan. With Megan she'd always been able to just be herself.

Now that was gone.

"Coming down here by herself was risky."

The flat tone in the coroner's voice stopped just short of insulting, but that somehow made the statement worse. He winced, as if he'd just realized how harsh he'd sounded.

"Sorry. Something like this, it's hard to take even if you've seen it dozens of times before."

The morgue, for all its stainless-steel and tiled-floor impersonality, suddenly seemed too small. Lauren made herself breathe out. *He's just here to do his job. Just answer the questions.* She worked to unclench her fists and failed. She wanted to defend Megan, wanted to explain how her sister loved life and new experiences, and she wanted to lash out at the coroner all at the same time.

"Megan was impulsive." The statement felt naked and indefensible to Lauren's ears. She desperately wanted to make the man understand, but she just couldn't find the words. There *were* words. She knew there were. "She wanted to see Jamaica. She's— *She'd* been going on about it for weeks. This trip was something she'd promised herself when she finished up a project at her advertising firm. This was a celebration. A getaway from the 24/7 life she'd been doing the last few weeks to close the deal."

"So there was no particular reason she came to Kingston?"

"She wanted to come here. For Megan, that was reason enough." Lauren thought back to her discussion with Megan before her sister had left. "There was some movie she'd seen lately. Something about an island cop." She shook her head. "I can't remember anything more than that. She caught a movie on Netflix, and she decided this was where she had to go." She took a breath. "That's just Megan. It's always been Megan."

The coroner made another notation in his book. "Was she meeting anyone down here?"

"No."

"Would she have told you if she was?"

"Yes. When Megan was in *discovery* mode, that's what she called it, she didn't want anyone else around that she knew. She said having a friend along was too limiting. It didn't let her really explore a new environment."

The coroner studied her with those gold eyes. "Would you say you and Ms. Taylor had a good relationship?"

It took a moment for Lauren to answer the question because her voice was thick and felt like shattered glass. "Yes. We did."

"You knew she was here?"

"Yes."

"Who else knew she was coming?"

"I don't know. Lots of people. Megan was people-friendly. That's why she was so good at her job. She kept a Facebook account and updated it regularly. She let everyone know she was taking this trip."

He wrote something else down. "So someone could have been meeting her here?"

"You'd have had to know Megan. If she knew something, or even thought she knew something, she told you. That's how she was."

"Did she have many romances?"

Heat filled Lauren's face, and she glared at the man.

"I didn't mean that the way it sounded. I apologize. That wasn't supposed to come out like that." He waited a moment to see if she would respond. When she didn't, he went on. "I just wondered if there's the possibility that she was currently seeing someone and you didn't know about it."

"No. Not that I'm aware of. Maybe Megan wouldn't tell me about a new guy in her life at the time that relationship started, but I always knew. Megan thought she could hide things like that, but she really couldn't. Not from Mom. Not from me. I knew." Lauren looked down at her sister and wanted to believe that. No, she *did* believe that. She would have known.

The air-conditioning unit cycled, and the cool air washed over Lauren. She wrapped her arms around herself and trembled slightly. Her fists still wouldn't open. She couldn't remember feeling so cold and so alone.

"If Megan had been meeting someone here, I would have known."

"You're certain of that?"

"I'm positive."

"Was Ms. Taylor casually seeing anyone back home? Someone that didn't come along on this trip?"

Lauren tried to keep up, but the questions just kept coming with staccato regularity. The man was like a machine. "No."

"There wasn't anyone she'd started seeing a little more of before she left? Maybe someone she was interested in but not officially seeing?"

"No. Like I said, with Megan, every potential romance was a big deal. I would have known." So would everyone on Facebook. Megan liked being in love. None of her suitors had stood the test of time, though. Megan had liked her diversions, but most of her exes were still friends of hers. That was just how she was. No one would hurt her.

Except that someone had. The dark bruising around Megan's throat testified to that.

"Was there anyone your sister had stopped seeing recently?"

"No."

"Anyone she'd stopped seeing in the past that would hold a grudge?"

"Look." Lauren's tone came out sharper than she'd intended. "You didn't know Megan. She wasn't like that. No one would want to hurt her. Not even an ex-boyfriend. She was the kindest, gentlest, most innocent person I've ever known." A tear fell from her right eye, and she felt it skid down her cheek. She refused to brush it away because she knew that would only open the floodgates.

"Where are Ms. Taylor's—" The coroner stopped himself and offered a correction. "Your parents?"

"We lost our father a few years ago. Mom's not well. She's gone through chemo and isn't able to travel. She asked me to bring Megan back home."

"I see. I'm sorry to hear that." For the first time, the cold, impersonal voice softened just a little.

Lauren took a deep breath and looked at the bruises around her sister's throat. They looked almost like handprints. "Can you tell me what happened to Megan? The police inspector I talked to on the phone wasn't very informative. I'm supposed to meet with him later." She didn't want to know what Megan went through in her last moments. She knew her mom wouldn't want to know, but they had to know so they would be prepared for what was going to happen next. For when whoever had done this was caught. "He said there's going to be an investigation."

"What were you told?"

Again with the questions. Lauren made herself breathe out. "A police inspector, Wallace Myton, contacted my mother and told her that Megan had drowned. When my mother told me, I knew that couldn't be true."

"Why?"

"Megan was a strong swimmer. And she didn't take chances out in the water."

"But you said she was impulsive enough to come to Jamaica on a whim."

Lauren's voice tightened and grew sterner. "I'm telling you what I knew the minute I was told what had happened. My sister did not drown."

He looked at his notebook. "I see that. You called Inspector Myton back and insisted that your sister could not have drowned. You wanted him to investigate your sister's death."

"That's right. The inspector was very polite, but I could tell he didn't believe me."

"He believed you after the bruises showed up postmortem on your sister's neck."

Lauren closed her eyes. She couldn't believe the man had stated that so coldly. "That's when the police knew Megan had been strangled."

"I'm sorry."

Keep breathing. Deal with this. Mom is count-ing on you. Lauren opened her eyes and looked back at the man.

"Did your sister know a magician named Gibson?"

The question came so far out of left field that Lauren couldn't help being surprised. "No."

The coroner looked puzzled. "Your sister didn't know Gibson. But I can tell by your expression that *you* do."

"I don't know him. I know *of* him. Everybody who loves magic knows who Gibson is. I've seen him perform." Lauren didn't like the way she suddenly felt guilty. That came from the coroner, not her. She grew more uncomfortable with the questioning, but she told herself she'd never dealt with something like this before and that her answers would help catch whoever had hurt Megan.

"What do you know about Gibson?"

That question was easier to answer. Lauren knew about Gibson. She answered automatically, pulling up the information effortlessly, and was grateful for the change of subject. "The man's a master illusionist. He's up there with David

Copperfield. Criss Angel. Doug Henning. Siegfried & Roy."

Frowning, the man shook his head. "I've heard of Criss Angel."

Lauren could tell from the coroner's reaction that he didn't care much for the magician.

"And I thought Siegfried and Roy were lion tamers."

"Magic is a part of their show." Lauren studied him. "I don't suppose you care for magic shows or magicians."

"Magicians are just another type of con artist."

Under other circumstances, Lauren knew she would have argued the point and maybe even gotten angry. Magic and illusion were an art, and shows depended on audiences wanting to be fooled just as much as on magicians and illusionists. For now, though, she just let it go.

"Why would your sister have been interested in Gibson?"

"I don't know that she was."

The coroner reached under the lab coat and took out a photograph. He held it so Lauren could see it.

In the photograph, Megan sat at a table in an

elegant club. She held a wineglass in one hand and looked as carefree as ever. The lights sparkled in her blue eyes, and Lauren knew her sister was having a great time. She didn't look frightened or under duress. Her smile was carefree.

The man sitting beside Megan was instantly recognizable. Gibson—that was the only name anyone knew him by—was a virtuoso of illusion. He'd had shows in Vegas and in Europe that were always sold out.

Dark and broody, a wild flip of hair hanging down into his face, Gibson looked mysterious and otherworldly. His persona, if it was a persona, never slipped. In the few interviews he'd done, he'd maintained his distance and hadn't revealed much about himself. No one knew where he came from. He'd just appeared on the magic scene almost as if by arcane means. If it was a shtick, it worked for him.

The black suit was Italian, neatly pressed, and fit him well. In the darkness of the club, he almost seemed to be disappearing into the shadows, as if the darkness around him was drawing him in under its protective wing. His was a hatchet face fleshed out by hard planes and deep-set eyes. A thin beard edged his jaw and pooled in a goatee around his thin-lipped mouth. The pale complexion made him look stark, as if he never saw the light of day.

Lauren had followed his career and had gotten to see him when he'd played at the Cadillac Palace Theatre in Chicago. Megan had bought the tickets and planned their whole night—including a blind date with an accountant for Lauren that was nice but didn't really have any spark.

"Is that Gibson?" The coroner jostled the photograph and broke the hypnotic intensity.

"Yes."

"Ever met him?"

"No."

"Your sister obviously knew him." He put the picture back inside his jacket.

Lauren didn't know what to say to that. She thought for a moment. "That picture wasn't on her Facebook page." She had looked at Megan's Facebook information and updates several times since she'd gotten the news about her sister. Until the night of her death, there had been constant updates and Tweets. "When was it taken?"

"The night she went missing."

Pain racked Lauren. "Megan was reported missing?"

The man nodded. "You didn't know that?"

"No." Lauren focused on her control. She needed to listen. She needed to learn. Her mom would want to know everything. "The first contact we had was Inspector Myton's phone call to tell us—to tell us Megan was gone."

"Your sister was reported missing."

"By whom?"

"A friend she'd made over the last couple days."

"What friend?"

The coroner hesitated, then answered. "A man she was supposed to have breakfast with the next morning. The guy called the police because he didn't feel like your sister was someone who would just stand someone up."

"Megan wouldn't. If she didn't want to go somewhere, she didn't go. If something came up, she called. That's just how she was."

"Then we have to assume she went with whoever did this to her."

Lauren looked down at her sister and shook her

head. "No. Megan would never go with anyone that would do something like this."

"Then she didn't know what the guy she was with was capable of."

"How do you know it was a guy?"

The coroner held up his hands. "Her killer had big hands."

An image of someone's hands around Megan's neck squeezing the life out of her nearly brought Lauren to her knees. She thought she was going to be sick. The room spun around her.

A strong hand took her by the elbow and lent her strength. "Easy. Just keep breathing."

Lauren did. She forced her legs to hold her up and concentrated on the door on the other side of the room till the room stopped spinning. "Did you find out where this man was when Megan went missing?"

"He was with friends. Iron-clad alibi."

Iron-clad alibi? What coroner talked like that? Obviously he had been watching too many cop shows. "If the police knew Megan was missing, why didn't they do something?"

"Adults come down to Jamaica to go missing all the time. There were no signs of foul play in her room. The police checked. She just didn't come back to her room that night."

Because she was dead.

"Normally three days have to pass before an adult is presumed missing." The coroner's voice was flat, but she knew he was trying to help her understand what had happened. "Since there was no evidence that she was abducted, the police kept on the lookout for her." He hesitated. "Things happen down in the islands. The police know that, too. Because they were looking, they knew who she was when they found her. Otherwise she could have been here in the morgue for days before anyone knew who she was."

That was a horrible thought. Lauren couldn't bear the idea of Megan lying here in this place of the dead for days without anyone knowing where she was.

The coroner's voice was lower, softer, and the Southern accent was more pronounced. "I'm sorry for your loss, Miss Cooper. But I'm going to get the guy who did this. For what it's worth, I can promise you that. He won't get away with what he's done."

The conviction in his voice startled Lauren. It

was raw and hoarse. She looked into those gold eyes and saw the stormy intensity of his gaze. She cleared her throat to make her voice work. "I'm sorry. I didn't get your name."

The morgue door opened, and a rotund man in his fifties stepped into the room with a file in one hand and a mug of tea in the other. He wore dark blue scrubs and a matching surgical hat. A mask hung loose around his neck. He gazed heatedly at the coroner standing beside Lauren.

"What are you doing in here, Detective Sawyer?"

The coroner ignored the older man and focused on Lauren. "Are you okay? Can you stand?"

Not knowing what was going on, Lauren drew away from the man.

"Never mind what you're doing here." The new coroner set his cup down on the nearby counter and grabbed the door. He pulled it open. "You're leaving. Get out of here."

The coroner—*Detective Sawyer*—looked at Lauren, tried to say something, then shook his head and left.

Lauren watched him go and didn't understand

anything that had happened, but she was going to find out. She headed for the door, hurrying to catch up.

Chapter 2

You're some piece of work, Sawyer.

Sighing in self-disgust, Heath Sawyer slipped out of the white lab coat as he strode down the hallway from the morgue. His long legs ate up the distance, but he couldn't get out of the building fast enough.

He'd wanted to see the dead woman's body himself, to get a feel for her and how she'd died. Whenever he was working a case, he wanted to know as much as he could about the victims. Seeing them at the crime scene or the morgue helped, but the trade-off was demanding. That kind of intimacy was a lodestone for nightmares. Years later, he could still remember the faces of the first case he'd investigated. He hadn't planned on running into the sister on this one.

But that didn't stop you from taking advantage of the situation when it presented itself, did it?

A wave of guilt assailed him, but he pushed it away. He'd learned to do that on the job, and he was on the job now, even out of his jurisdiction. Hell, he was out of his country.

Memory of the woman's perfume teased at his mind. Lauren Cooper was holding herself together better than a lot of grieving relatives Heath had dealt with over the years. In fact, she was holding it together better than he had when he'd found out about Janet.

He dropped the lab coat onto the counter where an older woman talked on the phone and entered data on a computer that had seen better days. A Bob Marley poster hung on the wall beside a calendar that said, Welcome to Jamaica. Have a Nice Day.

The woman narrowed her eyes, and her face pinched into a frown as she watched Heath. "Hey. Hey, you. You come back here and put that where it goes. I'm not your maid." Her island accent was thick.

Heath ignored her and headed for the stairs because they were faster than taking the elevator. He couldn't wait to be outside again where he could breathe. The island temperature was cooler than it currently was back in Atlanta, but the humidity was worse. He fished his sunglasses from his shirt pocket and slid them into place.

The area was dangerous, and that woman—Lauren Cooper—didn't look like someone used to dealing with dangerous situations. She had no business being at the hospital. The State Department should have taken care of the arrangements for getting her sister's body back to Chicago.

That image of her standing there beside her dead sister was going to haunt him. He felt guilty for having noticed how pretty she was. He didn't know what it was, but there was some indefinable quality about Lauren Cooper that had caught his attention.

Heath forced himself to keep moving. The woman wasn't his problem. She wasn't his responsibility. She couldn't help him because she didn't know what had happened to her sister. He was here looking for a murderer.

The man who had killed Janet.

As the pain and loss took him, Heath closed his eyes and tried to push it away. He had work to do, and he'd taken a leave of absence from the P.D. to get it done, to clear the ghosts from his head.

And he knew who his target was. Finally, in the picture of Megan Taylor, he had another link in the chain he intended to hang around Gibson's neck before he dropped the man into the ocean.

Let's see him magic his way out of that.

A trio of young nurses came down the stairs. They chattered in English and a smattering of other languages Heath couldn't identify. And they laughed as they talked about the party they'd gone to last night. He gave way before them and pulled to one side of the narrow stairwell. He nodded a silent greeting.

Then someone's hand dropped onto his elbow and yanked him around. He almost slipped on the narrow stairs, but his left arm came around, hand turning and curling over his assailant's wrist. The move broke the grip at once.

His right hand curled into a fist at his side, and his weight shifted on his knees as he prepared to throw a punch. The response was automatic, drummed into him from years spent on Peachtree and other violent streets in Atlanta while he learned his tradecraft in law enforcement. Mostly, he'd learned how to stay alive. And truth to tell, some of that willingness to hit came out of his Waycross, Georgia, roots, as well.

The identity of the person who had grabbed him surprised him.

Lauren Cooper no longer looked vulnerable and confused. Her dark eyes blazed with fury. Her black hair was cut close and followed the shape of her head down to her jawline and stopped just short of touching her shoulders. He remembered the style was called a bob, something he'd had to learn while taking witness statements.

She was beautiful. He'd noticed that when he'd talked to her in the morgue. Her sleeveless navy blue dress hugged every curve. Tiny silver hoops glinted at her ears, and a small silver cat pendant hung on the slope of just a hint of cleavage. Her mouth was generous, full-lipped, and her chin was strong and fierce. He hadn't noticed earlier, but there was a small spatter of freckles across the bridge of her nose. She wore short, black leather boots with buckles, and she looked as if she wanted to plant one of those boots where it would hurt.

As soon as that thought struck him, Heath turned sideways just a little, enough to hopefully allow him to block anything she might throw at him. He held up his hands in surrender. In his rumpled suit, one of the charcoal pinstriped numbers he wore on the job, he felt overdressed for the coming fight, but it had been enough to get him through the morgue staff.

"Who do you think you are?" Lauren reached out and grabbed him with both hands.

Pain ripped through Heath as he realized she'd grabbed shirt and chest hair, and he was pretty sure that was what she'd intended to do. "Hey, take it easy."

"Don't you tell me to take it easy. You just lied to me back there. Do you get off on doing that?"

Heath grabbed her wrists and tried to disengage her. "Look, I'm sorry. You don't know what's going on here."

"No. And you're going to tell me." Lauren set

herself and shook him. It wasn't hard to do. On the stairs he was off-balance, and there was the added problem of him not wanting to hurt her.

Heath scrambled to keep his balance, but one foot slid off the step, and he had to shift quickly to stop himself from falling. The woman was prepared for that. As soon as he moved, she yanked again, pulling him into her and backing into the stairwell railing. He knew her next move was to set herself again, twist and shove him down the steps. It was what he would have done. If he'd allowed himself to get in so close to a perp.

So he did the only thing he could do under the circumstances: he let go of her wrists and wrapped his arms around her, holding on tight. Her muscular body tensed against him, and he was surprised at her strength. She was five feet eight inches tall without the boots, and the low heels pushed her up another couple inches. She smelled sweet, a hint of vanilla and something else, some kind of berry. He was pretty sure of that, but his senses were swimming.

"Hey. Hey. Hold on."

"No." She pushed against him, but he held on

tightly. She tried to knee him, but he turned the blow aside with his thigh.

He put on his cop voice. "Miss Cooper, you need to calm down."

"I *am* calm." She pushed against him, harder. Her short-cropped hair flicked in his face as she struggled. An inarticulate scream ripped from her throat. Then she lifted her boot and drove the heel down his shin and into the top of his foot.

Pain burned the length of Heath's shin, but he held on to her, afraid that she was going to fall down the staircase and get hurt.

Two heavyset orderlies in hospital scrubs raced down the hallway. The woman at the desk urged them on, speaking in French or Chinese for all Heath knew. He was pretty sure it wasn't Spanish. He knew Spanish and Spanglish from the streets.

One of the orderlies grabbed Heath by the shoulders. "Let go of the woman, mon. Let her go now or I'm gonna mess you up."

The other man grabbed Lauren Cooper and pulled her back.

Heath released the woman, then shifted his arm under the arm of the man holding him and forced the man's grip over his head. The guy scrambled and tried for a new hold, but Heath spun around behind him, caught the guy's hand, and twisted it into an armlock behind the man's back. He held the orderly between him and Lauren like a shield. Pain drove the man up onto his toes.

"Okay." Heath made himself breathe normally. "We're all just going to take a step back. Take a minute. Think this through a little. Before somebody gets hurt." The man he held on to tried to break free. Heath moved the arm up just enough to let his captive know he could break it if he had to.

The other orderly hesitated, standing there looking uneasy.

Lauren wrapped her arms around herself and glared at him. She blew a strand of hair out of her face. "What were you trying to do in there? Why were you asking me all those questions? How could you do that to me?"

"Miss Cooper, those are all very good questions, and I respectfully decline to answer them. In a few more minutes, members of the Jamaica Constabulary Force are going to be here, and I don't feel like talking to them. It would be better if we could just agree that our meeting—timing and all—was a mistake."

"A *mistake?* I'm the only one who didn't know what was going on in there."

"Yes, and for that I'm truly sorry. I wish I could have made that easier, but I couldn't." Heath tried to think of something to add, but Hallmark didn't make a card for what he'd done to her. And trying to explain why he'd done what he'd done was just too involved. She didn't need to think about what he knew.

Besides, she needed to pick up her sister and get back home. She'd be safe there.

At least, Heath hoped she'd be safe. Gibson was still out there prowling, and the man was a predator. Heath was the only one who was convinced of that. Given the man's resources, he could disappear and strike anywhere he wanted to, then disappear again.

Losing Janet was proof of that.

Heath leaned close to his captive's ear and spoke softly. "I'm going to let you go now, partner. You just make sure that woman doesn't come after me. And if you come after me, I'm going to hurt you. Understand?"

Reluctantly, the man nodded.

"Good." Heath released the orderly and backed away. Three steps later, when there was no pursuit, Heath turned and fled up the stairs. The woman didn't come after him, and he was a little surprised at that. She didn't seem like the type to give up.

Back at the fleabag hotel where he was staying, Heath took the hotel key card from his shirt pocket and swiped it through the reader. The lock made a *thunk* and the light cycled green. He put his hand on the doorknob and drew the snub-nosed .357 Magnum from a holster at his back. He'd bought the revolver off an eleven-year-old boy shortly after he'd hit Kingston four days ago. Guns were easy to get. It was answers that were hard.

For a moment, he just held on to the door handle and listened. Nothing moved inside the room. That didn't mean anything. Neither did the electronic lock. The hotel wasn't a security showcase. That was one of the reasons he'd checked in after he'd found it.

Cautiously, he pushed the door inward and followed it inside the room. The hinges squeaked just a little, but he liked that. Besides the *thunk* of the lock, he also had the squeak as an early warning system.

A quick sweep of the room revealed that no one was waiting for him. The hair trapped between the second drawer down and the frame of the chest of drawers told him no one had searched the room.

He locked the door behind him, holstered the pistol, and got down to business. He took off his jacket and threw it on the unmade bed. If maid service was available in the hotel on a daily basis, the sign on the door would keep them out. Maybe. He didn't like leaving anything to chance.

His shin still ached from where Lauren Cooper had scraped him with her boot heel. He cursed softly at the discomfort, but he didn't hold the action against her. He'd deserved everything he'd gotten and probably more.

In the bathroom, he raised his pant leg and surveyed the long, bruised and bloody scrape down his leg. Lauren hadn't been messing around. She'd known exactly what she was doing. *Good for her.*

He returned to his unpacked suitcases and took out a small medical kit. Methodically, he cared for the scrape. On the island, with all the heat and the potential for disease in some of the areas he was traveling in, there was a good chance of infection.

He returned the medical kit to his suitcase and took out a small wireless printer. After plugging the unit in to the wall, he took out his phone and brought up the images of Lauren Cooper he'd taken while she'd been grieving over her dead sister.

At the time he'd taken the pictures, he'd felt like a heel. Now, looking at the woman's grief-stricken face, he felt even worse. As a police detective, he'd seen more than his share of devastated people, physically and emotionally. He'd been told that in his job as a homicide investigator, he was always meeting people on the worst day of their lives.

Heath sent the pictures over to the printer and

took them as soon as they'd come through the unit. The Lauren Cooper he saw in these shots didn't mesh with the wildcat who had met him full-on there on the stairs. He tried to think of how many women he knew who would have tried something like that. There weren't many.

Janet would have. She'd fought her killer. But in the end it hadn't done her any good. He'd killed her just the same. In fact, Gibson had probably enjoyed the struggle.

Realizing the black anger was about to consume him again, Heath pushed it away. He couldn't let that happen. The anger was raw and vicious, worse than any drug an addict could crave. When the anger was in bloom within him, there wasn't room for anything more.

He'd learned that as a kid at Fort Benning, Georgia. His father had been a drill instructor for the army, stationed at the post. Heath had had to take a lot of grief as a teenager, and he hadn't always chosen wisely. For him, the world was black-and-white. That view of things had led him into the military and into the police department later. He loved being a detective, balancing the scales a little every time he broke a case.

He'd learned to put away the anger, but since Janet's death, it was back with a vengeance.

He went to the small closet and reached up for the ceiling. Gently, he pushed and popped out the section he'd cut the first night he'd stayed in the room. In the darkness that filled the closet, the cut he'd made couldn't be seen.

Reaching up, he took down the roll of canvas he'd bought from an art store on his way to the hotel. Walking over to the wall near the small desk, he unrolled the canvas and tacked it to the irregular surface. The canvas was three feet wide and eight feet long. The dimensions weren't those of the whiteboard he generally used in the detective bullpen, but the canvas gave him plenty of room to work.

Photographs from crime scenes and printouts from reports were secured to the canvas with double-stick tape. The seven women stared out at him from their pictures. All of those shots were from before Gibson had finished with them. All of them had a photo of a black card with an embossed white rabbit on them. They'd been sent to the various police departments within days of the discovery of the murders.

Below them were crime scene photographs. Some of them were bloody. Sometimes, and the profilers attached to the murders didn't know why, the killer liked to cut his victims. Other times, like with Megan Taylor, he just killed them.

Muriel Evans, the weather girl in Newark, New Jersey, had been shot through the head.

Tina Farrell, the masseuse in Los Angeles, had had her neck broken in a manner that suggested Special Forces training.

The Taylor woman had been the first to get strangled.

The White Rabbit Killer didn't seem like a disorganized killer. He was too methodical, too good at what he did. But an organized killer often used the same weapon. Like the knife.

Janet had been tied up and thrown into a hotel room shower, then had a naked electrical cord dropped in after her. Her death hadn't been easy. Heath still smelled her burned flesh in his nightmares.

So far, the White Rabbit Killer hadn't killed the same kind of victim or in the same city. Not even in the same state. The serial killer was a traveler, but he took some kind of pride or satisfaction in his kills because he always left a calling card behind: a black card embossed with a white rabbit.

At first, no one in the media or in the homicide squads that were investigating the murders knew what the white rabbit meant. Janet had been the first detective to match the white rabbit to the magician Gibson. She'd been the one who'd discovered Gibson had been in all of the cities of the victims during the time they were killed.

But there was no evidence linking Gibson to the murders. And now, even with Janet among the victims, there was still no evidence.

The killer's pace was picking up, though. Only two weeks had passed since he'd killed Janet. His timetable was picking up speed. Either he was growing more confident, or whatever he got from murdering women wasn't lasting as long as it had.

Heath took the pistol out and placed it on the desk. He reached into the small refrigerator near the desk and took out a beer. The air-conditioning in the room was weak and he was already sweating.

In the center of the canvas, Gibson stared out with those malevolent eyes and that mocking smile.

Heath sipped his beer and considered his next move. Gibson was on the island. He stayed locked away somewhere up in the hills. No one Heath had met knew for certain where, and the local police force wasn't being overly helpful in finding the man. They had no reason to interfere with the man's privacy. Or maybe they didn't know.

Gibson wasn't wanted in Jamaica, and he wasn't wanted by anyone in the United States, either. At least, not yet.

Heath's cell phone buzzed for attention. He took it from his pocket and glared at it. The unit was a throwaway he'd gotten in Atlanta before leaving the city and didn't have caller ID, but he knew who it was. Only one person had the number.

Cursing, Heath took the call. "Yeah."

"How's it going down there?" Jackson Portman sounded totally relaxed, but then he always did. An ex-football player and African-American, Jackson's build and don't-cross-me demeanor made him look more like a movie heavy than a homicide detective.

"It's too hot."

"Can't be no hotter than 'Lanta."

"Did you call for a reason? Or are we just gonna talk about the weather?"

"You busting any heads yet?"

"No. Why?"

"Got a call about you."

"From the locals?"

"Nope. I already talked to them. Inspector Myton don't look like he's gonna be a fan of your work anytime soon. Said you had no business bein' up in their business."

"I've heard Myton talk. He doesn't sound like that."

"That's 'cause I'm paraphrasing."

Heath took another sip of his beer. "If it wasn't Myton that called, who was it?"

"A woman. When I first heard her voice a little while ago, I was hopin' maybe you met somebody."

"Overnight?"

"I ever tell you how I met my first missus?"

"Too many times." Heath sat up straighter

and looked at Lauren Cooper's picture. "Let me guess who the woman was."

"Sure."

"Lauren Cooper."

"Shocks me how you know that, bro. I mean, you should be a detective."

"I'm working on it. Myton must have told her about me." Heath took another sip of beer. Or the coroner told her. He hadn't cared for Heath, either.

"I don't think so."

"Why?"

"She knows too much about you. Stuff Myton wouldn't know."

Heath stared at the pretty woman in the picture. He'd missed something about her. "Like what?"

"Where you lived. About your sister and her kids. About your gym membership. About me. A lot more than I know about you, actually. That's why I thought maybe you'd hooked up with someone down there and just didn't tell me. Then I realized it was you I was talking about, and I thought maybe I'd call you, check that out.

Now you sound like you ain't any too happy to hear from her."

For a second, Heath felt a faint tickle of fear. His sister and his two nephews lived not far from him in Atlanta. He'd been helping out with them when he could since her husband had left her. "I'm not."

Jackson waited a beat. "You want to tell me how Lauren Cooper knows so much about you? Especially if you ain't all chummy and everything?"

There was a knock at the door.

"I'll call you back." Heath picked up the .357 and got up. He walked to the door and avoided the peephole. Quietly, he slid the cell phone into his shirt pocket, then dropped a hand onto the door handle and popped it open just enough to see out into the hallway.

Lauren Cooper stood there with her arms folded. "We need to talk, Detective Sawyer. Now."

Chapter 3

"Are you alone?"

That wasn't the response Lauren expected from the man. She'd expected him to be contrite or defensive, or at least surprised, maybe even outraged that she'd found him, but he didn't seem to be anything more than irritated.

"What?"

"Alone? Are you alone? It's not a hard question to answer." Heath stepped through the door and glanced out at the courtyard in front of the motel room. He held a gleaming black revolver in his right hand, tucking it close behind his thigh so it couldn't easily be seen.

"Yes. I'm alone." Even as she said that, Lauren wondered if coming here alone was intelligent.

Now she was wishing she'd gone to the local police. But she also realized that course of action probably wouldn't have gotten anything done. Heath Sawyer might have been there on police business, and even if he wasn't, he hadn't broken any major laws.

Heath grabbed her by the elbow and tugged her through the doorway. Lauren set her heels and started pulling back. He glared at her. "You came to see me, lady. I didn't come knocking on your door. So either leave or come in. This door isn't staying open."

For a moment, Lauren seriously considered turning around and leaving. That seemed to be the path of least resistance. Except that she'd just seen her murdered sister and she wanted some answers that she felt certain the man in front of her had. Inspector Myton hadn't had many. Then she spotted the canvas spread out on the wall behind Heath.

On autopilot, Lauren stepped into the room, barely aware of Heath shutting and locking the door behind. She kept walking, taking in the photographs and police reports secured to the canvas thumbtacked onto the wall. Her gaze slid over the images of women who were obviously dead, all of them taken at crime scenes.

Then her eyes found the photos of Megan. A feeling of vulnerability descended over her. Sharp pain shot through her stomach. She closed her eyes and took a breath.

Heath crossed over to the canvas and took it down. Despite the speed at which he moved, he was careful with the photos and reports. "I'm sorry, Miss Cooper. You shouldn't have had to see that."

She turned to him. "You're a cop."

His eyes narrowed slightly. "Not a cop. I'm a homicide detective. Something like what happened to your sister? I'm a professional. I'm the guy you call when something like this happens."

Focus, Lauren. She made herself breathe out and put distance between herself and the pain. "Who called you about my sister?"

He hesitated. "Nobody."

"You were here four days before my sister was murdered." Lauren had gleaned that from the receipts in his wallet, which she had pilfered during the physical altercation they'd had at the hospital.

Heath nodded warily, no doubt wondering how she'd known that. "I was."

"Why?"

"I took some personal leave that I had coming. Thought I'd see the sights."

"Did you know she was going to be killed?"

The question rocked him on his heels. Despite his efforts to remain calm, Lauren saw that she'd caught him by surprise.

"No. How could you think something like that?"

"It's a lot easier than you think. Especially since the masquerade in the morgue."

"I went there to get information."

"About what?"

"About whoever killed your sister."

"I thought you had that figured out."

"I believe I do."

Lauren pointed at the rolled-up canvas. "Then tell me what's going on. Explain to me what my sister's picture is doing on that. Tell me who killed her."

He scowled and walked over to a small table surrounded by three chairs. He raised the beer bottle he'd liberated from the small refrigerator in the corner of the room. "Can I get you a drink?"

"No."

Heath sat in one chair and put his feet up in another. He sipped from the beer bottle. "I really would like for you to leave. What's it going to take to make that happen?"

Folding her arms over her chest, Lauren ignored him, keeping her focus on the rolled canvas. She felt confident he wasn't going to try to physically remove her from the room. He'd have already done that if he'd wanted to. And she was certain he didn't want to have anything to do with the local police after the confrontation in the morgue. The actual coroner had been very vocal about Heath's presence there. "Do you think Gibson killed Megan?"

After a brief hesitation, Heath looked at her. "Do you want me to lie to you? Because what I think doesn't matter." The note of sarcasm in his voice surprised her. At first she thought it was directed at her, then realized it was more personal than that.

"I want you to be honest with me. If you can."

"I can. And I think Gibson killed your sister.

Getting someone else to believe that can be difficult. I know. I've tried." He frowned. "A lot of people, evidently, aren't prepared for that kind of honesty."

Even though she'd asked for the answer, the words hurt. Lauren wasn't as ready to hear them as she'd thought she would be. Still, she kept her composure. Being weak in foster homes wasn't something that let a kid survive. She'd learned to keep her emotions inside and present that hard shell to the world.

"I'm sorry." Heath blew out a breath.

"It's fine."

"No, no it's not. A person shouldn't have someone taken away from them like that."

Lauren heard the note of wistful hurt in his words, and she knew that she wasn't alone in her pain and misery. As a foster child, she'd learned to read tones and expressions and body language at an early age. That was part of the self-preservation tool set. "Who did you lose?"

The wince and the slight hunching of his shoulders, like a boxer who had just taken a blow, let her know her instincts had been dead-on. This wasn't just a case to the detective. "A friend."

Lauren nodded toward the canvas. "Is she on there, too?"

He ran a big hand across his stubbled jaw and took a breath. He didn't bother looking at the canvas. "No."

"Why not?"

"Because that's a visual victimology. My friend doesn't belong with those others. When Gibson killed her, it was different."

"What was different?"

"The motive for the murder. Gibson made Janet's death personal because she'd made her pursuit of him personal."

"How did he make it personal?"

Heath leaned back against the wall. Green flakes stirred restlessly in those gold eyes, but he looked tired. She hadn't noticed that earlier in the coroner's office. Looking at him now, seeing him better, he looked slightly pale beneath the new redness from the sun.

"We worked a homicide in Atlanta. A real-estate agent. Thirty-two-year-old mother of three."

"'We?'"

Heath drained the rest of the bottle and set it on the window ledge. "Yeah. Janet and me."

"She was a police officer."

"Detective. Like me. She was working as lead on the Celeste Morrow murder, working the case with her partner. She used me as a sounding board. We did that for each other when we caught cases where we got stuck and needed an outside opinion. Janet let me have a look at the case." He stared at the wall, but Lauren knew he wasn't seeing it. "We both knew the serial killer was a sociopath. All the traits were there. Random killings. Nothing tying the victims together. But the killings were usually savage."

Memory of the crime scene photos on the canvas played inside Lauren's mind. There had been so much blood. "My sister was drowned. She didn't die like those others."

"No. She didn't. But I learned that Gibson's name came up in the investigation."

"He was identified by the picture she took with him."

Heath nodded. "I've been monitoring Gibson, trying to stay up with him, but he vanishes whenever he wants to."

"Inspector Myton doesn't think Gibson had anything to do with Megan's murder."

"How do you know that?"

"I asked him. He didn't come out and say it, but he let me know he thinks you're obsessed and perhaps not in your right mind."

Heath smiled disparagingly. "Inspector Myton isn't interested in ruffling any feathers, Miss Cooper. People die down here all the time. Sometimes they're Americans. Myton accepts that. Part of the cost of doing business. Eventually all of that goes away. If Myton can catch someone red-handed, if that someone isn't so connected that they're practically untouchable, he'll put that someone behind bars. I'm convinced that's the truth." Heath looked at her. "The problem down here is that money plays. That's the name of the game. If someone has enough money, they can get away with murder. And a guy like Gibson has plenty of money." He paused. "He's clever, too. Otherwise he'd never have gotten to Janet."

Lauren wondered if the two of them had been involved. It wasn't unheard of, especially with the kinds of hours police personnel worked. She wasn't going to ask, but something must have shown on her face.

"We were just friends." Heath looked a little

embarrassed, then hurt followed. "Actually, we were more than that. Janet was my FTO. Field training officer. She worked with me when I made detective. She got me started on my investigations, and she was there during some rough patches."

"I'm sorry for your loss."

"Yeah. Me, too."

Outside the window behind Heath, street noises filtered in. People walked by. Cars passed on the streets, rubber squeaking on hot pavement. Someone upstairs was playing the television or a music system too loud.

"How old was she?"

Heath scowled. "What?"

"How old was your friend? If she trained you, she must have been older, right?"

"Eight years."

"Making her forty or so."

"About that." Heath's eyes narrowed, and he looked at her with increased interest. "Janet doesn't fit on that victimology board because she called Gibson's lawyers and left a message saying she knew what he was doing, that she was going to stop him." Pain turned his voice hoarse for a moment. "I didn't know till afterwards. The lawyers' number turned up on her cell phone records." He drew in a breath. "Gibson killed Janet to prove that he could do it under our noses and get away with it." His voice turned hard. "But that's not going to happen. He's going to pay."

Desperately, Lauren sought to turn the conversation away from Heath's dead friend. She was afraid that he would shut down, and right now she wanted—*needed*—information about Megan's death. "The other women on that—" she pointed at the rolled canvas "—are in their twenties."

"Yeah." Heath sat up a little straighter and looked as if he was regrouping. "They are. Like your sister. Gibson has a thing for younger women. He's older—"

"Forty-three. I know."

He focused on her with new intensity. "How do you know so much about him?"

"I know magic."

"Sure you do."

Still annoyed at Heath and wanting to wipe that smug look off his face, Lauren put her left hand to her temple and closed her eyes as she tilted her head back. "Think of your address."

"You're joking."

"No. I'm going to read your mind."

"You're a mind reader? I didn't know mind reading counted as magic."

Using her right hand, Lauren palmed Heath's driver's license from the wallet she'd taken from him earlier. She opened her eyes, took her hand away, and looked at him. Then she gave the address she'd noticed on the driver's license earlier.

He studied her with indolent eyes, not saying anything.

"Well, is that your address?"

For a moment, he didn't say anything. The defenses went up. She saw that in the way he held his shoulders, the way he tilted his head to look at her. "How do you know so much about me?"

"Like I said, magic." Lauren raised her right hand, palm forward so he couldn't see the driver's license trapped by its edge between her first two fingers.

"I'm not a big believer in magic."

With a flourish, Lauren shook her hand and his driver's license appeared at the end of her fingers. For a moment, Heath didn't know what to say. Before he could recover, she flicked her wrist and sent the plastic rectangle spinning at him.

Surprisingly, like a cat snapping a moth out of the air, Heath caught the license in his left hand. After he perused the plastic rectangle, his eyes turned to slits. His free hand slid down to his pants pocket, then he looked shocked. "You picked my pocket and stole my wallet at the morgue."

"I *borrowed* your wallet." Lauren reached into her pocket and removed the article. She tossed it to him. Before she'd arrived at his hotel room, she'd photocopied all of the documents at her hotel and left the copies tucked away in her room. Heath knew a lot about her. It only seemed fair that she have the same opportunity.

With the same easy skill he'd shown in catching the license, Heath caught the wallet. He glanced through it quickly. Satisfied that everything was there, he shoved the wallet into his pocket. His eyes narrowed. "Picking pockets isn't a skill most people have."

"It's just a riff on sleight of hand stuff. I work at a magic store."

"Where?"

"In Chicago."

"You sell magic tricks?"

"Yes. I guess you don't know as much as you think you do, Detective Sawyer." Lauren hated that Heath's lack of knowledge about the field made the shop sound pedestrian. "But they're not the kind of tricks you'll find for some kid's birthday party. Professional magicians come there to buy equipment, to talk with each other, and to design new illusions."

Heath leaned his head back against the wall, relaxing a little, or maybe only providing a deception. "Has Gibson ever been there?"

"No."

"Why? Is he that good?"

"I don't know. The guy just appeared on the scene one day and streaked to the top of the heap. A lot of people want to know where Gibson learned his craft. If anyone knows, if anyone is helping craft his illusions, they're not talking."

A frown twisted Heath's features. "People have been trying to figure that out?"

"Sure. The guy's a celebrity in a field where secrets are prized. Every magician wants to know what's in every other magician's bag of tricks. Especially if that magician is as successful as Gibson. The fascination for magic only gets deeper if you're actively involved in the field."

"I'll take your word on that." Heath leaned forward in his chair, dropping his feet to the floor and resting his elbows on his knees. "You've never met Gibson?"

"No."

"Your sister hadn't, either? Until the other night?"

Lauren thought for a moment. "Not that I'm aware of."

Heath nodded. "Somewhere, somehow, they crossed paths. I'd like to know if it was just here, or if it was somewhere else."

"If nothing connects the victims you say Gibson has killed, what makes you so certain he is the killer?" Lauren couldn't believe she was asking that question so calmly, but at the moment she felt dead inside. All of the hurt and pain was pushed back, waiting in the distance like gathering storm clouds. The anger was still there, though. She wanted to know who was responsible for what had happened to Megan.

"Janet and I talked about this case for weeks. I can't even remember which of us came up with Gibson, or how we tripped to the fact that Gibson was playing in each of the cities where those victims were killed. We'd starting checking newspapers in those cities during the time periods of those murders. We found Gibson."

"If you were looking in the newspapers, you probably found a lot of overlapping things."

"We did. But Janet liked Gibson for it."

"Why?"

Heath's lips tightened for a moment. "She was good at what she did. She could make creative leaps that other detectives never got to. Sometimes you get a serial killer who kills over a wide range of areas. Usually he turns out to be a sales rep, or maybe a long-haul trucker. We even considered that, but nothing fell into place. Then we found Gibson. And everything fit. Especially the White Rabbit card."

"Like a magician pulling a rabbit out of a hat."

"Yeah. The guy enjoys playing his sadistic little games. It's his signature. He claims his victims."

"Then why didn't you go after him?"

"We couldn't. We tried making our case to other law enforcement departments, but nobody wanted to go after Gibson. Everything was circumstantial and he wasn't even in-state anymore. Chasing after him would have been expensive, and police departments have budgets that television cop shows don't have to worry about. We couldn't prove that Gibson had any kind of contact with any of the victims. No sightings, no meetings. No forensic evidence. Nothing." Heath looked at her. "Not until that picture of him with your sister. That's the first concrete clue we've had. And it's down here in this place where I have no jurisdiction."

"What are you going to do?"

Heath shook his head as if to clear it and stood. "No more questions, Miss Cooper. I shouldn't have told you as much as I have, but I felt I owed that to you." He folded his arms over that broad chest, and she could still see the lost hurt shining in his eyes.

"You came down here before Megan died." Lauren kept her voice level. "You had a plan then."

"I still do." Heath walked to the door and opened it. "Time for you to go."

Lauren wanted to stay and argue, but she also wanted to stay and comfort him, and be comforted. Detective Heath Sawyer was the only person she knew in Jamaica. She didn't want to be alone, didn't want to have to go back to the hotel room and talk to her mother, but she knew she had to do that. She was already late in doing it.

And she had to make arrangements for taking Megan home.

She nodded and walked to the door, pausing only a moment to look at Heath. "Thank you for being honest with me. It…helps."

He winced at that but didn't say anything about his earlier duplicity. "Have a safe trip home, Miss Cooper."

She turned and walked toward the elevator.

* * *

Downstairs and out of the building, Lauren slid behind the steering wheel and set her purse in the passenger seat. She felt the vibration of her phone inside while she was reaching for the keys to the car. She checked the caller ID.

Mom.

She hesitated only a moment, then put the phone back in her purse. She knew her mom would be worried, but Lauren didn't want to try to talk to her until she was in her hotel room. There, at least, she would have some privacy.

After sliding the phone back into her purse, she glanced back at the hotel room where Heath Sawyer was staying. The curtain was pulled slightly to one side, and his profile shadowed the light.

Resolutely, Lauren put the car into gear and pulled away, but she couldn't stop thinking about Gibson. Imagining him as a serial killer seemed like some kind of fantasy.

So was the idea of never seeing Megan again, but that one was dark and terrifying.

Chapter 4

At the window, Heath watched Lauren Cooper drive away and vanish into the dark streets, only realizing then how late it had gotten. Only a few blocks over, a neon fog pooled above an area near a beach where the tourists gathered. Over there the music would be too loud, college kids and twentysomethings just out in the world would be dancing and celebrating summer, beer and liquor would flow, and no one would know that the White Rabbit Killer had taken another victim.

Maybe knowing wouldn't even slow them down. They were there to party.

Pensive and irritated, Heath thought about grabbing his jacket and heading out into the cool night, just blowing through an evening by trying to sink into the magic of the island. That would have been wasted effort, though, and he knew it. If things went well, he'd only end up more restless than ever. If things went badly, he could end up in a fight. He knew himself, and he knew the dark mood he was in.

It had been years since he'd exhibited that kind of behavior, but he knew he was next door to it now. He could feel the techno trance of the club music in his veins. That was where he would gravitate to. Trance, industrial heavy metal, something that would bang through him, something that would amp him up even more.

Country music would be worse. Those songs were loaded with pain, and he'd do his best to drown it. He'd done it before. The only reason he'd become a cop was because he hadn't known what else to do after four years with the Marines right out of high school. He hadn't wanted the military life his father still enjoyed, but he'd wanted something physical, something where he'd make a difference. He'd taken the police exams, thinking that if the cops didn't want him, he'd re-up with the military.

Atlanta P.D. had taken him, though, and he'd found work that he could do that wasn't the same thing day in and day out. He didn't see himself as a hero. He was a guy who helped paint that thin blue line between the civilians and the savages. He'd liked busting heads, maybe a little too much.

Detective Janet Hutchins had taken an interest in him. She'd seen that he had an eye for investigation, didn't just take the first answer he was given, and that he checked the facts. She'd gotten Heath groomed for his detective's shield, then partnered with him for three years till he made Detective 2nd and got a junior partner of his own.

That was two years ago. The junior partner had been Jackson Portman.

Heath turned away from the window and pulled out his cell phone. He pulled Jackson up on speed dial, then punched the call through. It rang only once before the connection was made.

"There you are." Jackson sounded relieved.

"Here I am."

"Thought you were gonna leave me hanging just when things were getting interesting."

"No."

"You still got company?"

"No. I need you to do something for me."

"Sure. First, tell me about Lauren Cooper. That's how this favor thing works. You do something for me, I do something for you. How did that woman know so much about you?"

"She read my mind."

Jackson snorted derisively. "Bro, the stuff she knew, even you don't know without checking. What's your gym membership number?"

Heath didn't say anything because he didn't know it. Case numbers he knew, phone numbers of snitches he knew, but not so much numbers involving his personal life.

"Well? Time's ticking." Jackson whistled, an off-key version of *Final Jeopardy!*

Heath grimaced, knowing that once Jackson was armed with the facts of what had happened, his partner would never let it go. "Back at the hospital when I was checking out the murder down here, I bumped into Lauren Cooper. She's the dead woman's sister. While we were in a heated discussion, she lifted my wallet."

"Lifted your wallet." Jackson sounded hollow, as if he couldn't believe what he was hearing.

"Yeah, it means she picked my pocket."

"I know what it means. Just surprised you'd slip up like that. It ain't like you, bro." Some of the colloquial accent was gone from Jackson's words. He was deadly earnest now. "You really don't have your game, Heath. You should come back home. Let's sit down and sort this out. We still own one of the White Rabbit murders."

"Two. We own two." Neither of them mentioned Janet's name.

"Come home. We have enough to buy into the investigation and leverage some muscle from the captain. Let's dig into it together. If I have to, I'll get some leave and we'll work the investigation together."

"The investigation is down here. This is where Gibson goes to hole up. He's got a place down here. I found it. I just can't get close to it."

"All right. That's something we didn't know. How did you find his place?"

"Gibson made a mistake. The dead woman took pictures of his house and uploaded it to her Cloud. I got a chance to look at the data dump from her iPad, accessed the pictures, and found the house."

"So he took the woman to his house?"

"Yeah."

"Can't the locals get a search warrant?"

"Gibson says he put the woman in a cab, waved goodbye, and he never saw her again."

"Uh-huh. And they decided not to press him on that?"

"They don't have any proof that that wasn't what happened."

"They find the cab driver?"

"No."

"They look?"

"Myton says they did, but this is a tourist area. A lot of people take cabs every night."

"You think the locals are protecting him?"

"They're being careful. Gibson is rich. They don't want to ruffle any feathers until they have a lock."

"You did mention this guy is a probable serial killer? Probably gonna kill again?"

"Yeah. The cops here I've been talking too aren't big fans of the American justice system, and they're even less happy about Georgia detectives wandering in off their beats to poke around in their business."

"That would be a problem. So tell me about Lauren Cooper. Did she look hot to you? 'Cause from what I'm looking at here, she looks seriously hot."

"Can I quote you on that to your future second missus?"

"Lord, no. That woman's jealous enough."

"What are you looking at?"

"Her file. Since she called in, knew so much about you, I thought it was only fair we know stuff about her. Only expected to get a hit on her from the Chicago DMV. That's where she told me she's from. Turns out she's had a little bit of a record."

That surprised Heath, but then he thought about how easily she had picked his pocket. Even on his worst day, he wasn't the easiest guy to pull something like that on. "What record?"

"Breaking and entering and assault. From what I see, she broke into a guy's apartment and punched him out in Chicago three years ago."

"For what?"

"Says here she claims the guy stole an illusion she was working on. She's some kind of magic designer or something. The guy claimed that they came up with this thing together, that there wasn't a clear title to anything. The judge dropped the hammer on her because it was a home invasion. She ended up doing some community service—magic shows at old folks' homes and orphanages—and had her record expunged. Are they serious about the magic thing?"

"She does magic."

"She must be good at it if she can lift your wallet. 'Course, her looking like she does, I could see how you got distracted."

Heath ignored that. "Actually, the magic angle is what I want you to look into. Gibson picked up the woman down here. She'd taken her sister to a magic show Gibson put on in Chicago. Check and see if any of the other victims had a connection to magic in any way. Maybe Gibson is culling from a more select group than we thought."

"Looking for relatives of people who jones on magic?"

"Yeah."

"I'll have a look." Jackson hesitated for a moment. "Something you told me when you first started training me to work homicide—stay detached. Look at everything from the outside. The minute you crawl inside of an investigation, you lose all perspective. I'm gonna tell you now, because you're my friend and I love you like a brother and you're likely gonna be my best man when I wed my second Missus Portman, that you're all kinds of up inside of this investigation. The captain came out asking what did I know about you impersonating a coroner. I told him I didn't know nothing."

"I can't be detached from this one. Gibson killed Janet. Look into those cases and let me know what you come up with regarding the magic angle." Heath broke the connection and tossed the phone onto the rumpled bed. He got a fresh beer from the refrigerator and stood at the window looking out again, trying to figure out what his next move was going to be.

Instead, to his surprise, he couldn't keep his thoughts away from Lauren Cooper and how she'd felt struggling against him. He closed his eyes and could smell that berry vanilla scent again. Then he forced his eyes open and sipped his beer.

There was a thread here. Nobody killed that clean. He was going to find it, and he was going to use it to strangle Gibson.

"There." From the backseat of the Jaguar X351, Gibson pointed at the low-rent hotel off the beaten path of the city. "Pull into the parking lot."

In front of him, behind the steering wheel, Roylston resettled his bulk, looking like a steroid-infused earthquake in motion. Dressed in a black business suit, his skin dark and his head shaved, he could have passed for a native to the island. Only the Boston accent marked him as an outsider. During the three years he'd been with Gibson, Roylston hadn't ever spoken much, and never mentioned anything personal. As far as Gibson knew, the bodyguard/chauffeur didn't have a life outside of protecting him.

But all three of the live-in security special-ists who tried to manage Gibson were like that. None of them wanted to get to know him, and they didn't want him to know anything about them. They got paid to watch over him, protect him and try to rein in his "impulses."

Escaping the watchdogs that had been with him throughout his life had been the initial part of the Game he played now. He'd avoided his protectors when he was a boy, escaped them at times for glorious bits of freedom, but in the end he'd always let them catch him in order to satisfy his father. Even at forty-three, Gibson didn't want to completely escape his father's attempts to control him. That was the very best part of the Game.

That particular thrill was even better than the killing, which he relished.

The bodyguards tended to be compliant with him. They didn't want his father to know when they lost him, so they covered up most of his escapes—except for the ones that were too egregious.

His father covered for him as well, trapped by his desire to keep his corporation protected and to have an offspring to carry on his name. Gibson had robbed the man of that as well by choosing his stage name. Still, his father held out foolish hope of someday controlling him.

The man was trapped, simply couldn't let go of the selfish dream.

That was the very best part.

Roylston glanced up at the hotel. "This is where that Atlanta detective is staying."

The fact that the man knew so much of his business irritated Gibson. He rested his elbows at his sides, curled his elbows and steepled his fingers under his chin. "I know that."

With obvious reluctance, Roylston guided the sedan into the parking lot. The headlights flashed against the parked cars in the lot. "This is dangerous."

"Of course it's dangerous. I wouldn't visit if it weren't dangerous. The circus doesn't really come alive until the aerialists perform without a net, until the lion tamer sticks his head inside a lion's mouth. Death hovers there, just a *snap* away. And the potential of that is what keeps the crowd on the edges of their seats." Gibson smiled and leaned over to the window so that he could look up.

Atlanta Detective Heath Sawyer still stood at the window. His shadow was a blurry image behind the curtain.

"You know I'm close, don't you, Detective?" Gibson smiled at that thought, savoring it because he knew that closeness was making the man's wounds hurt even more. When Gibson had killed the female detective in Atlanta—*Janet,* her name rolled so invitingly across his tongue—he had known her death would push the man to go the distance. Gibson had considered killing both of them, but in the end he'd decided not to. Having a *mortal enemy* was a delightful concoction that he'd never thought of.

Heath Sawyer didn't worry Gibson. He had lawyers and riches that would keep the police far from his door. And if the man got too bothersome, it was never too late to take care of that loose end.

After a couple of minutes, the shadow at the window went away.

Gibson waited for a short time longer, enough to make Roylston uncomfortable. Then he leaned back in his seat again and addressed the driver. "Let's go."

Roylston had the sedan rolling within the next heartbeat. "Any particular destination?"

"Downtown, I think. I want to see how the

revelers are doing." Gibson took a California ten dollar gold piece from his pocket and rolled it across his knuckles. The coin leaped and flew like it was a living thing. He closed his hand on the coin, folding the fingers in with his other hand, then opened his hand again to reveal that the coin had vanished.

He smiled at the smoothness with which he worked. He was good and he knew it. The Atlanta detective could disappear just as easily when the time came.

Until then, there was the Game to play.

Back in Lauren's hotel room, the phone call to her mother didn't last too long. Chemo wore her out and left her in a fog. Plus, it was so late that Lauren had woken her up when she'd called. Her mother had insisted that she call when she returned to her room. Their conversation had been sad and groggy and disjointed, and had finally trickled off when her mother no longer had the strength to maintain it.

The doctors said she was improving, that this round of drugs was battling the cancer back into submission. She wasn't supposed to undergo any stress during this time. That wasn't going to happen.

After leaving Heath Sawyer's room, Lauren had had to return to the morgue to finish paperwork she'd left undone earlier when getting to know more about Heath Sawyer. She'd worked in a numb state, just plodding through the information, borrowing a computer to get information she didn't know, and contacting the insurance company as well as the State Department.

All of that had been exhausting.

Now, she couldn't sleep, and it was two o'clock in the morning. She kept seeing Megan laid out on that table, so impersonal, so still, so cold to the touch. But the memory was confusing because Heath Sawyer was also there. No matter how hard she tried, she couldn't get the man out of her mind. She could still feel the strength of him when she'd fought him, still see the indomitable will in his green-flaked gold eyes and the set of his stubbled chin.

But she remembered the pain in them, too, when he'd told her about his old partner. Lauren remembered that image of him the most, that vulnerability that she'd seen that she was sure he would deny.

There was something more behind that pain, though. Heath Sawyer had been hurt somewhere else along the way, too. She could sense it in him even though she couldn't yet put her finger on it. It was the same way she could take apart an illusion. Something was there just behind the curtain. If she spent enough time around him, she would have it.

That was why many of the illusionists who frequented Mirage Magic in Chicago where she worked insisted on giving private shows for her as they perfected pieces of their performances. If they could fool her, they could fool anyone.

Lauren didn't think that was true, but it was nice to hear.

Warren Morganstern, the semiretired magician who had started the business over forty years ago as a supplement to his performances, told her that she had an eye for magic. More than that, though, she had a love for magic. She wanted to believe that magic could happen, and that made all the difference.

Seven years ago, when Lauren had been in college, she'd answered an ad in a newspaper for a part-time position at the magic store. When Megan had found out about it, she'd teased her unmercifully, till Lauren had finally gone and applied, knowing she was going get turned down, just to shut her sister up.

Then magic had happened. Lauren had gotten the job at Morganstern's shop. She'd never asked how many other people had applied or what had made her application stand out among the others. Seven years later, she had taken over the store, allowing Morganstern to completely retire from performing, though he kept active in the business to socialize with the other magicians.

Since Lauren had started working there, she'd also started booking some of the acts, and she'd gotten successful at that. After a couple of years, she had doubled the store's business, and Morganstern was giving serious thought to moving to a larger building.

Lauren hadn't thought of the job as permanent, but she couldn't think of anything else she'd rather do. She loved magic. She loved the possibility of what-if.

For a while, she tried to relax and go to sleep.

Her flight tomorrow didn't leave till the afternoon. Her mind wouldn't stop spinning with everything that had happened.

Finally, she gave up trying to sleep, sat up in bed and got her laptop computer out of the bag. She logged on to one of the community boards that she used for the magic store and started asking questions about Gibson.

Someone out there had to know who the man was. Lauren still didn't believe the man had killed Megan, but someone had. Heath Sawyer seemed to be the only person really digging into the investigation. Lauren thought that if she could prove the killer wasn't Gibson, maybe Heath's attention would refocus on the case from a different perspective.

Lauren was not going to let the killer go free if she could help it.

Wearing skintight surgical gloves, Gibson took out one of the specially embossed cards he'd had made when he first decided to kill. Ordering the cards anonymously from Thailand was simple. He'd used a drop box at a box store, an online pay service that accepted cash up front, and ordered from a large printer that did a lot of volume in special jobs. He knew the police investigators had tried tracking the origin of the cards he'd sent to claim his kills, but they hadn't been able to do that.

Still seated in the rear of the luxury car, with Roylston looking on, though he was pretending not to, Gibson played with the card. Even with the gloves on, his skills were amazing. The card appeared and disappeared with lightning quickness.

Tiring of the game, he slid the card into an envelope he'd gotten straight from a box, affixed the address label he'd cut from an image he'd downloaded from the police department's website. He added a picture of the young woman who'd been recently killed, a picture of her in the water not far from where her body had been discovered by two young Germans looking for a romantic section of the beach. He pulled the paper from the sticky strip, made sure there were no fibers clinging to it, and sealed the envelope.

When he was finished, he waved to Roylston, who pulled over to the public mailbox in front of the seedy hotel where Heath Sawyer was staying. Gibson thumbed down the window and leaned out for just a moment, knowing there were no security cameras on the premises to catch him in the act.

He popped the letter through the slot, then sank back in his seat as Roylston guided the car through the parking lot like a big shark. Gibson hummed to himself and took out the gold coin again, rolling it deftly across his knuckles, almost mesmerizing himself as the gleaming metal caught the reflection of the neon lights.

Chapter 5

You shouldn't be here. Heath told himself that again and again as he stood on the fringe of the crowd at the graveyard service. *You should be back in Jamaica trying to find Gibson.*

In the end, though, he'd had to come to Chicago to attend the Megan Taylor funeral. Part of the reason he'd felt the need to be there had to do with the investigation. The other part was the guilt that he still felt for deceiving Lauren Cooper. He didn't know how he was going to make up for that, so he concentrated on the investigative area.

Once the police departments in the various cities had realized they were working a serial killer after the White Rabbit cards had started coming in, they'd gone out to the victims' families and friends and gotten as many pictures and as much video as they could. They'd combed through those images and video footage, the same way he and Janet had done.

No one had ever seen Gibson.

That didn't mean he hadn't been there, though, and it was that hope that had brought Heath to Chicago.

At least, that was what he told himself, but he knew he wanted to see Lauren Cooper again, as well. The woman had left quite an impression on him.

She sat there beside the coffin with an older woman that Heath assumed was her mother. The woman appeared frail and exhausted, leaning on Lauren for physical and emotional support. Big sunglasses crowded the woman's face under the broad-brimmed hat. Heath had noticed the lack of eyebrows and the wig at first sight and had known she was taking chemo.

Beside her, dressed in black, her head bare and bowed, Lauren held the older woman's hands in one of hers and wrapped her thin shoulders with her free arm.

It was a good day for a funeral, which was an odd thing to think, Heath admitted to himself, but he did. He'd attended many funerals when it had been raining or so muggy you could drown in your own clothes. The sun was shining, the trees were green and vibrant overhead, blocking the early afternoon sun and dropping a green tinted haze over the cemetery. A gentle wind blew to stir things up, but even then the grounds were quiet enough that the preacher's voice rang out.

A lot of people had turned up for the funeral. That was one of the things that Heath had noticed during his attendance at the funerals of murder victims, and of his own family. There were always more people at a young person's funeral than at an older person's burial. Common sense said that an older person would have made more friends and more solid relationships. In actual practice, more people attended the funerals of the young.

Death was a new experience for young people, and it was scary at the same time. They didn't know how to act, and when an older person passed, they were always a generation or two away. Death didn't seem so close. So they came to funerals because it was a social event and because it was something new.

Now you're being cynical. Heath took in a breath and let it out. He was tired. He still wasn't sleeping well because the frustration clamored inside him. But over the past three nights, the last one in Jamaica and the two since, he'd had nightmares, too. He still had the ones involving Janet, but Lauren Cooper was in there now as well, and he didn't know why.

The worst one had been when he'd stood by helplessly while Gibson put Lauren into one of those boxes magicians always used, locked her down tight, then broke out the chain saw. In practice, magicians routinely passed swords, guillotines and chain saws through those boxes. No one ever got hurt, though. But in the dream, Lauren had screamed in pain, and blood had cascaded to the floor. Heath hadn't been able to save her.

A creeping chill climbed Heath's spine. He was dressed in a black suit, fitting in with the other attendees, but he suddenly found himself wishing he'd brought a jacket.

And a gun.

His own sidearm was back in Atlanta, and the revolver he'd bought in Jamaica was still there in that hotel room behind the air vent cover. Getting a pistol while in Chicago was too problematic.

He'd slept in his rental car down the street from Madeline Taylor's home. That was where Lauren had been spending her nights. She had her own apartment, but she'd stayed with her mother. Heath had gotten a police scanner from a pawn shop and tuned it in, then grabbed as much sleep as he could during the night while watching over the two women. In the mornings, he'd tailed Lauren as she'd gone about making arrangements for her sister's funeral.

He'd gone back to stakeout mentality, sitting on a person of interest and hoping for the best. There was no reason to think Gibson would be there, but the killer's habits were accelerating and no one knew why. Sometimes they just did. The adrenaline rush the killer got from killing wore off faster and faster.

Taking shelter behind the tree where he stood, Heath raised the small digital camera he'd brought with him from Jamaica, part of his investigation go-bag he had for when he had to move fast. He focused the camera quickly and took another round of shots, getting as many of the faces as he could. He'd get more when the people came by to pay their last respects at the grave. Identification would come through Facebook and online college and high school yearbooks.

"Hello." The voice came from behind him, neutral but authoritative.

Heath knew at once that he'd been busted. Slowly, keeping his hands on the camera, he turned around.

Two men, one black and one Hispanic, stood there just far enough apart that they couldn't both be gotten easily, but they were still right there to help each other. Neither of them had their hands on their guns, but their jackets were open, and their hands were open and ready.

"Hi." Heath released the camera with one hand but kept the now-empty hand up and clearly visible.

"I'm Detective Green with the Chicago police department." The black man's eyes were invisible behind black Ray-Bans. His hair was cut short, barely showing against his skull. A small, narrow mustache framed his mouth. "This is Detective Hernandez. We need to see some ID."

Heath didn't bother asking why. If he'd been Green, he'd have asked him for identification, too. In fact, in different instances on some of the cases he'd handled, he had asked to see identification from people who hadn't seemed to fit at funerals and other events.

"Sure, Detective. Right-hand pants pocket. I'm going to move slow."

The man nodded.

Heath forked his wallet out and passed it over.

Green opened the wallet, then looked at Heath again. "Says here you're from Atlanta. You're a long way from home."

"I've got some more identification for you if you'll let me get it."

"Slow."

This time Heath reached inside his jacket and brought out his badge case. He passed it over. Green flipped it open and found Heath's shield.

"What are you doing here, Detective Green?"

"The deceased was the female victim of a violent crime. Those go down, usually it's the husband, a boyfriend or an ex. Sometimes a family member. A funeral can bring out the worst in people. The captain thought we might drop by, make sure everybody stays safe." Green looked up. "Are you on the job here, Detective Sawyer? Something the Chicago police department should know about?"

"I've been working the White Rabbit killings."

Green nodded toward the funeral party. "This was one of those?"

"Yeah. Jamaica P.D. hasn't made it official yet, but it is. They got the card two days ago."

"I haven't heard anything about it."

"Jamaica has better control over their news services than we do here."

"If they can keep that quiet, they do." Green handed the wallet and badge case back.

"It won't last forever."

"No, it won't." Heath put away his things, managing it one-handed because he was still hanging on to the camera.

"Does the family know?"

"I told the sister when I met her down in Jamaica. I don't know if she believes me."

"You tell her about the card?"

"No. I haven't talked to her since Jamaica."

"Probably something you should do."

Heath hesitated. "We didn't really get on while we were down there together."

Green lifted an eyebrow, but he didn't ask about that. "Tell you what. I'll call Jamaica, confirm the White Rabbit connection, then I'll have a word with the sister. Professional courtesy."

"I'd appreciate it."

"If you find out anything further, Detective Sawyer, let me know." Green passed across a business card, pausing briefly to write a cell phone number on the back. "Looks like we're all interested in this now. I've been following the White Rabbit case and know what happened in Atlanta."

Heath took the card and slipped it into his jacket pocket.

"I'm sorry it went down like that with your detective."

"Me, too."

"But you must have been getting close to the guy, right?"

"We thought so." Heath knew he couldn't drop

Gibson's name. The department would rake him over the coals for exposing them to a lawsuit like that.

"We'll get this guy." Green gave Heath a brief flicker of a grin. "It's what we do." He nodded and kept moving, his partner a silent shadow behind him.

Keyed up all over again, face-to-face with how Janet had been lost so quickly, Heath tried to put his emotions aside and concentrate on doing his job. When he turned back, though, he saw that Lauren Cooper was headed straight for him, and she didn't look happy to see him.

At first, Lauren hadn't believed that Heath Sawyer was there. She'd noticed the police detectives as they'd been circulating the funeral. She didn't know what they were doing there, or if someone from the police department always showed up in a situation like this, but she knew that Heath Sawyer shouldn't have been there.

From the disappointed look he gave her, she knew he wasn't happy that she had seen him. For some reason, that lack of appreciation made her angrier and more confused. She had felt livid, surprised and excited to see him all at the same time. That was something she didn't want to do. Her emotions were too confusing now.

He cleaned up really well. The black suit was clean and pressed and fit him nicely. It made him look a lot different than he had in the casual business attire he'd worn while masquerading as a coroner. He was clean-shaven, his hair moussed and in place, and the pair of Oakley sunglasses would have gotten him on the cover of *GQ*. His tie was knotted perfectly.

Lauren stopped in front of him and folded her arms, looking up at him.

Heath gave her a small, crooked smile. "By the time I realized you had spotted me, it was too late to retreat."

"Do you feel the need to retreat, Detective Sawyer?"

"Yes, ma'am." His Southern accent was more pronounced now, or maybe she was so used to the native accents around her that something different really caught her attention.

"What are you doing here?"

"Miss Cooper." He spoke calmly to her, and that infuriated her even more. She was burying her sister, and he was butting in, catching her off guard the same way he had down in Jamaica. "Maybe this isn't the best time to talk about this."

"Did you have another time planned?"

"No."

"You came here because you thought Gibson would be here, didn't you?"

He hesitated a moment before answering. "I did."

Lauren sipped her breath and made herself speak rationally. She glanced over her shoulder to check on her mother. Madeline Taylor was doing fine at the moment, having some final words with her brothers and sisters. The closeness of those family members had made Lauren feel the slightest bit out of place, something she hadn't experienced in years.

She looked back at Heath. "I read over the newspaper stories about the White Rabbit killings. All of them. They're all different. Different women. Different ways they were killed. Different times of days, weather conditions, a lot of things are different. I've also done a lot of reading on serial killers the last few days."

Heath didn't say anything to that.

"Most serial killers kill the same kind of victim in the same way with the same kind of weapon. The killing is an orderly series of events." Lauren couldn't believe she was talking so nonchalantly about such a horrible subject. The reading had been hard, but she'd always been good at research.

"There are different kinds of serial killers." Heath's voice was flat, no-nonsense. "What you're describing? Those are ritualistic killers. Guys who have hang-ups about something or a particular kind of person. There are also compulsion killers. Guys who don't know why they kill other than whatever satisfaction they derive out of it. Gibson is an organized killer, always in control of the victim, in control of the encounter area. He plans out his killings, but he doesn't do the same thing over and over again." He paused. "Magicians don't always pull the same tricks over and over again, do they?"

Lauren thought about that, surprised by the question.

"I've seen some of those guys work when Janet and I first started looking into Gibson as our doer. Some magicians work the same patter and stunts. Some try to come up with new acts every time you see them. But it's all about the magic, about the performance."

"Do you think that's what Gibson is about? The performance?"

"You know his magic better than I do. Which kind of magician is he?"

It only took Lauren a moment to realize that Heath had a point. Gibson did a round of shows, then he dropped out of the public view. When he reappeared months later, he had a whole new elaborate production ready to go. Sometimes the show was intimate magic for a group or a pay-channel broadcast. Other times it was escapology, a feat that taunted human endurance or even death itself, such as when he'd sat in an immersion tank for over seven minutes before breaking free of his shackles. He was well short of other magicians' time, but anytime a feat like that was done, it was impressive. The pay channels had eaten it up. Another time, he'd levitated himself in an effort to get out of a notoriously haunted house that burned down around him while malign spirits tried to keep him within the fire. Lauren didn't believe in malign spirits, but the performance had been nerve-racking all the same.

No one knew what Gibson would do next.

"He doesn't like to repeat himself."

Heath didn't say anything to that.

"You could be wrong, you know." Lauren spoke pointedly, getting her words across like hammer blows. "You're focusing on Gibson because he was in a photograph with Megan. The whole time you're doing that, telling Inspector Myton that Gibson is Megan's killer, the real killer could be getting away."

Heath's clean-shaven jaw bunched, and the muscles stood out in sharp relief. His words were soft. "Gibson is the killer, Miss Cooper. Maybe if more people believed me, we could put him where he belongs more quickly. Either way, I'm going to get him. You can bet the farm on that."

"There's nothing to tie Megan to the White Rabbit Killer."

He hesitated. "Yeah, there is. Two days ago, Inspector Myton received a black card with a white rabbit embossed on it. The Kingston police just aren't telling anyone yet." He looked past her. "You should go back to your mom. She probably needs you."

Looking over her shoulder, Lauren checked on her mother and saw that most of the family members had gone. She couldn't just leave her mother sitting there at the gravesite. Hurting and feeling guilty about being gone so long, she turned back to address Heath.

Only he wasn't there. He was already several long strides away from her, moving with deceptive speed through the graveyard.

Lauren considered going after him, but she didn't know what else to say. He was set on his course, and there was nothing she could do to break him of that.

He's not your problem. She concentrated on that, then turned and walked back to rejoin her mother.

Chapter 6

"You need to eat, Lauren. I can fix you something if you'd like."

"I'm all right, Mom. You should rest. Or, if you're hungry, I can make you something." Lauren perched uneasily on the edge of the couch in the living room where she'd spent the best years of her life. She didn't know what to do with herself. She was exhausted from the funeral, but she knew she couldn't rest. Thoughts of Megan's murder and Gibson kept whirling around inside her head. And Atlanta, Georgia, detective Heath Sawyer was in those thoughts way too much for any degree of comfort.

"No, honey. I'm fine." Her mother didn't look fine. The days since Megan's murder had sapped energy from her that she didn't have to spare. Her skin was pale and blotchy. Now that they were back home, at the house where Lauren had finished growing up in, her mother had taken off her wig, pulled on a crocheted cap to cover her bald head and sat in her favorite chair.

The television was blank, but the street noise drifted in through the closed windows. Outside, children played in yards, celebrating the arrival of summer and the end of school. Lauren didn't have many of those memories of playing in the neighborhood at that age. She'd been older when she'd arrived, but she could remember the other, younger kids in the neighborhood doing that. Whitman Park was only a couple of blocks away.

Lauren sat on the couch and felt alone. As heavily medicated and as tired as her mother was, she was barely there. The pain between them was so raw that it couldn't be touched.

After a little while, her mother slept in the chair. Unable to sit there any longer, Lauren got up quietly and retreated to the kitchen to fix a cup of tea. It felt good going in the kitchen, finding everything in its place where it had always been.

What was unaccustomed was the silence. Even after her dad had passed away, there had always been joy in the house. Megan had been the center of it, of course, because she had been the chatterbox. Lauren hadn't realized how silent the house could be without her sister.

The tears came while she waited for the water to heat. For a time, she let them fall, grateful that she'd been composed throughout the service. She didn't like showing emotions in front of others. She'd never felt comfortable doing that.

A few minutes later, the kettle whistled. She took it from the stove and dried her tears, then filled a cup and added a tea bag. As she waited for the tea to steep, she walked through the house, finally going upstairs to the rooms she and Megan had lived in when they'd been there.

Megan had been the first to leave, the first to get a "grown-up" job because Lauren hadn't been able to let go of the job at the magic store. She hadn't been ready for freefall among strangers then, and magic was—and still remained— her passion. There was something about magic, something about the illusion of being something else, or maybe *someone* else, that appealed to her in ways nothing else did.

Megan's room had been a mess after she'd departed in a whirl of excitement, littered with cast-off clothing, keepsakes from junior high, high school and college, books and rock star posters. It had taken Lauren and her mom three days to clean everything up, and they'd threatened to box it all up and send it to Megan to deal with, but neither of them wanted to think about finding the boxes sitting in Megan's apartment unopened when they went to see her.

The bed was neatly made. Trophies lined one wall. Pictures of Megan as a cheerleader, a business leader and in speech competitions, as well as on family trips and vacations, covered the wall. A person could stand in the middle of Megan's room and watch her grow up in the spotlight. Lauren had always thought that was weird, the growing up part. As for the spotlight part, there just hadn't been any other place for Megan.

Lauren's room, on the other hand, had been freshly cleaned and neat the day she'd left it. She'd stayed in the house till she'd gotten through college, to help her dad with her mom's first bout with cancer. Then, when the job at the magic store had become full-time, once Mom's cancer was in remission, Lauren had moved out and claimed her own space.

Even four years later, that apartment still felt like a temporary way station, a brief shelter from the turbulence that had claimed the rest of her life. Nothing before had been permanent.

This, this had been home. And now it was withering away.

She sat on the edge of her bed and glanced at the walls. Compared to Megan's, they were empty. The Taylors had adopted her when she was eleven, young enough that she could share a lot with Megan, but old enough that she could never really escape the experience of getting shuffled between foster homes.

Pictures of her at that age and older were on the walls. She'd played softball and ran track and swam competitively. All were sports more or less recognized for individual effort. Only in the family photos did she look like a team player, and that was primarily because Megan had always been right there to pull her in.

On the chest of drawers, Lauren's early magic

kits sat in boxes and pouches, as if a magician would be along any moment to put them to use. Lauren was surprised that her mother hadn't thrown them away, but Mom had always maintained that magic was the one thing that seemed to make Lauren come alive. A magician had to have an audience, she'd always said, and that was when Lauren had shone.

Lauren had let her believe that was true, but the actual truth was that she had sat in her room and performed magic all the time. Megan had watched in fascination at times. On other occasions, Lauren had used her tricks to bother Megan when she was on the phone. Especially after she developed an interest in boys. It was hard to focus on a conversation when coins and scarves and other small items kept appearing and disappearing.

Walking over to the chest of drawers, Lauren picked up the white-tipped black magic wand. It had been her first. When it was popped the right way, it became a bouquet of flowers. When she'd been eleven, she'd thought it was the coolest trick ever.

Now she just wished it had real magic in it so she could bring Megan back.

"What do you know about Gibson?"

Warren Morganstern lifted his head from the deck of cards he'd been shuffling and regarded Lauren. He was in his seventies, comfortably possessing a potbelly and a wrinkled face that still showed all the handsomeness of the posters Lauren had seen of his magic days. His hair was iron-gray and neatly parted on the left. Laugh wrinkles surrounded his blue eyes. He wore a pressed white shirt with the sleeves rolled up to midforearm. His jacket dangled from the back of his chair. A steaming cup of coffee sat to his right on the small table.

He eyed Lauren. "How are you doing, kiddo?"

"I'm okay." Lauren leaned on the load-bearing pillar behind the table. She knew she didn't look good. She hadn't slept well last night. Her mind was too full of Megan and Gibson and Heath Sawyer. Everything was getting twisted up in there.

"You don't look okay." Morganstern's voice was gruff and hoarse, an old man's voice now and not really strong enough for stage shows. He still had the hands and reflexes of a master, though. He just needed an assistant who could carry on the verbal part of the act. Lauren had been that assistant a number of times.

"Thanks."

"I call 'em like I see 'em, kiddo." Morganstern waved at the chair on the opposite side of the small card table.

The magic store had four little rooms where magicians could rehearse tricks and illusions. In those rooms they could practice with the tricks to see if they would work for them, or they trained with other magicians to make the trick their own.

After a brief hesitation, knowing that Morganstern was wanting to talk to her and knowing that she didn't feel like talking to anyone, Lauren went around the table and sat.

Morganstern shrugged. "I thought about coming by, after the funeral."

"I'm glad you didn't."

"I know. You always liked to be alone with the hard stuff." Morganstern shuffled cards again. "Your mom okay?"

"With the cancer or with Megan?" Lauren knew she sounded angry. She *was* angry, but she didn't mean to take it out on Morganstern.

He didn't flinch, though. He'd known her too long. "Both."

Lauren let out a tense breath. She loved that she didn't always have to be polite with Morganstern, and that he didn't take it personally when she wasn't. "She's doing okay."

"You asked about Gibson. I'm assuming we're talking about the magician, not the guitar." His eyes twinkled just a little.

"Yes."

"Something on your mind?" The cards danced in Morganstern's capable hands, flitting from palm to palm like flickering doves.

"I need some time off."

Morganstern nodded. "Sure, sure, kiddo. Me and the missus expected that. That's why I'm here this morning. Take all the time you need. We cleared our schedules, not that there's much to clear these days. That's what retirement is all about." He smiled.

"I don't know how much time that will be."

Morganstern shot her a curious look. "It's okay." He paused. "You just do what you gotta do."

Lauren paused, not knowing how much to tell him. Warren Morganstern was a good man. He'd looked out for her for years, another father figure, but this one had led her into a realm of make-believe possibilities and a way of forgetting so many of the bad memories.

"One of the last people Megan saw down in Jamaica was Gibson."

Morganstern nodded and reshuffled the cards. He laid them on the table in a row, then made them dance from side to side. "How'd that happen?"

"I don't know."

"Did Megan tell you about it?"

"No."

"Seems like that's something she would have told you about."

"It is. I think she just didn't get the chance to."

Morganstern nodded and was somber and silent for a moment. "Something must have happened pretty quick for her not to tell you something like that."

"I know."

"So you're wanting to talk to Gibson? See if he knows anything about...your sister?"

"Yes."

Morganstern shrugged. "Gibson isn't exactly a helpful man. As far as I know, he doesn't have any friends. No one in the business here that I know, and I know a lot of people."

"But he has a home down in Jamaica?"

"Rumor would suggest so. He spends a lot of time down there."

"Why?"

Morganstern sighed. "I don't know, kiddo. Most magicians like a place they can retreat to in order to design their illusions. Operate under the radar till they get the bugs worked out. I can make a few calls, see what I can find out."

Lauren nodded, getting more comfortable with her course of action. She couldn't sit back because the police weren't obviously going to carry the investigation very far. "I need this to be kept quiet. I don't want Gibson to know anyone from the magic community is looking into him."

"All right." Morganstern frowned. "I gotta say, I don't like the idea of you going down there and talking to that guy. Especially not if you think you gotta do everything on stealth mode."

Lauren looked at him and saw the worry in his face.

Morganstern hesitated a moment, then started talking. "Ten years ago, when Gibson was just starting out on the circuit, before he blew up and got network attention with those street magician YouTube spots, he had a reputation for being hard on female assistants." He shrugged. "That doesn't make him a killer, but I don't think he's a nice guy, either. You've seen what fame does to some people—makes them think they're living in a whole different world than the rest of us."

"You think that's what Gibson believes?"

"I don't know, kiddo, but I think it's something you should keep in mind. And now that I think about it twice, this is probably something you should tell the police about and just walk away."

"I'm not going to do that." Lauren was silent for a moment, thinking about Heath Sawyer and his vendetta. "There's a police detective from Atlanta. He lost a friend, another police officer, to the White Rabbit Killer."

Morganstern's eyes narrowed. "You're saying Megan was murdered by that guy?"

"It hasn't come out yet, but the local police handling the investigation in Kingston have received a White Rabbit card."

Morganstern swore softly.

Lauren went on, divorcing her emotions and speaking mechanically. "Heath and his friend had worked the White Rabbit murders together, and they were narrowing the focus on Gibson. Everywhere one of those murders was committed, Gibson had been playing a venue."

"Have the police questioned him?"

"No. They don't have any evidence against him, nothing that ties him to the murders."

"Then why are you so interested in Gibson?"

"Because he was one of the last people to see Megan alive. He could have seen something that will lead the police to the killer."

"If that was the case, why doesn't he come forward?"

"Maybe he doesn't know he saw anything. Maybe he doesn't want the publicity. Either way, he's got enough lawyers to keep the police away from him."

"What are you planning to do?"

"I want to ask him about that evening he spent with Megan. I want to know where they went, who they saw, anything that might help with this investigation."

"You're not an investigator, kiddo."

"I know. But Heath Sawyer is, and he appears to be a dedicated police officer. He's blinded himself, though, totally focused on Gibson."

Morganstern shook his head. "You can't do that. You focus on the magician, you miss the trick."

Lauren reached across the table, took the deck of cards from Morganstern and shuffled them. "We know that. That's why I want to go back down there and talk to Gibson, find out what he knows. I think if anyone can find out who hurt Megan, Heath Sawyer can do it. I just want Heath looking at everything." She raised the cards in a tight stack in one hand, then made pulling motions with her other hand.

As if by magic, one of the cards levitated from the deck. The new card was one of a collector card series featuring magicians. This one was of Gibson, showing him in his patented black leather jacket and black turtleneck. A white dove nested in his cupped palms. He was stone-faced, mysterious, and no one could tell if he was going to release the dove or break its neck in the next moment. Lauren had never thought that before, but she did now, and the prospect chilled her.

Morganstern grinned in appreciation then clapped. "Good job, kiddo. I never saw you slip that card into the deck. Very smooth."

"That's because you were focusing on the magician."

The next day, Lauren boarded a flight that was going to be the first leg of her return to Kingston. She stored her carry-on in an overhead bin and took her seat next to the window. She preferred sitting there because she got the most privacy.

She opened her iPad and brought up one of the books she'd bought on the subject of serial killers. After her meeting with Morganstern, she'd returned home, found her mother resting, and spent the evening getting familiar with the books available on the subject. If Heath Sawyer was right about Megan being murdered by a serial killer, Lauren wanted to know more about the murderer.

She'd read for hours last night, wishing sleep would come, then had been taken by surprise when she'd been awakened by her cell phone's alarm chirping into her ear. After a hasty good-bye, she'd left her mother in the house with a promise to return soon and no word at all of where she was going.

Trying to go back home or to work was out of the question. Her mother believed it was that strong sense of responsibility that had propelled Lauren through life that had made her leave. If she'd known where her daughter was actually headed, Lauren knew her mother would have held on to her.

At least, there would have been a huge fight and lots of tears on both sides, because Lauren couldn't let the issue go. The horrible death Megan had suffered wouldn't leave her thoughts.

After takeoff, Lauren settled in and read as much as she could. The author reduced the socio-pathic savagery inherent in most serial killers to a clinician's report that held almost no emotion. According to the author, law enforcement personnel who chased serial killers had to learn to tune out their own feelings.

She couldn't help wondering how police investigators could shut down emotionally like that. Heath Sawyer certainly hadn't, and Lauren was willing to bet his ex-partner hadn't, either.

Or maybe things were different when the killings were personal.

Lauren quickly negated that, as well. Heath Sawyer had been involved in the hunt for the White Rabbit Killer before his friend's murder. Reading the newspaper reports of the murder last night had left Lauren shaken, but she'd also gained a greater understanding of Heath's motivation.

The White Rabbit Killer hadn't been satisfied with killing Detective Janet Hutchins. The murderer had ensured the funeral would be a closed casket service. Some of the photographs associated with the story had featured Heath Sawyer in them, as well.

One of the things that had surprised Lauren was the amount of dedication "organized" killers devoted to the craft. Those killers pursued, "trolled" for victims of a specific type and tended to repeat their crimes, doing them over and over again as if seeking perfection. In fact, according to the book, that need to reach a "perfect" murder compelled some of the murderers.

Lauren couldn't help but think how similar that single-minded purpose was to a stage magician planning out the perfect performance. That thought disturbed her because she could see how someone like Gibson might fit the profile. She had made a list in the notes function on the iPad, then quietly ticked them off.

She rolled her neck and suddenly became aware of a familiar cologne. Her pulse sped up, and she felt self-conscious. Trying to remain casual, she glanced over her shoulder and caught Heath Sawyer leaning on the overhead bin and looking down at her.

He wore jeans and a dress shirt with the sleeves rolled to midforearm. His hair looked as if he'd run his fingers through it with a little mousse and hoped for the best. Stubble gleamed on his chin. Fatigue showed in his face, but his gold eyes gleamed as the green flakes moved restlessly.

"That's not exactly light reading there, Miss

Cooper." His voice was flat and carried an accusatory note.

Lauren pressed the home button and shut down the tablet. She didn't have anything to say, and she wasn't going to give him any ammunition to work with.

After a moment, when he realized she wasn't going to answer him, Heath frowned. "Do you mind telling me where you're headed?"

The trip had a flight change. "Yes."

Heath waited, but she didn't answer. "Yes, what?"

"Yes, I do mind. Very much."

Heath dropped into the unoccupied seat.

"Happy?" Lauren tucked her iPad into the pouch of the seat in front of her.

"To see you? No. You're not stupid, that's why I can't believe you're acting that way." Heath took in a breath and let it out. "Going back down there is the worst thing you can do."

"Really? And where are you headed? I'm betting it's not back to Atlanta."

Heath took in a deep breath, and she knew he was holding back his instinctive response. "If you go after Gibson, you might get hurt."

For a moment, Lauren almost softened. He was worried about her. Despite all the anger and frustration that he was feeling, she believed his concern was real. But she couldn't back off. "According to you, no one can get close to Gibson. So why worry?"

"Your sister got close to the guy."

A sharp stab of pain lanced through Lauren and momentarily took away her breath.

"Look." Heath ran a hand through his hair. "I'm sorry. I didn't mean to go there." He sighed. "What I'm trying to say is that your mother has already lost one daughter. She shouldn't lose both of them."

"She won't." Lauren knew it was pride that made her say that, but she wasn't going to be made afraid, either. She wasn't going to take chances. Not like Megan had.

An older airline hostess with elegant makeup and a no-nonsense attitude parked herself in the aisle beside the seat Heath had taken. She folded her hands in front of her and gazed steadily at Heath. "Is this man bothering you, miss?"

"No, I'm not bothering her. I'm trying to save her life."

The hostess glanced at Lauren. "She doesn't appear to be in any jeopardy. We have an air marshal riding this flight with us. If you don't return to your assigned seat, I'm going to get him."

Growling inarticulately, Heath heaved himself up from the seat and walked to the rear of the plane.

The hostess peered at Lauren. "Will you be all right? Is there anything I can get you?"

"No. Thank you. I'm fine."

The hostess hesitated for just a moment longer, then retreated.

Leaning back in her seat, Lauren concentrated on breathing and relaxing. But she kept thinking about Heath, his intensity and his desire to capture his friend's killer. She hadn't realized it before, but she knew then that she was afraid for him.

"She's there?"

"Yeah, I'm looking at her now." Heath stood in the middle of the crowd at baggage claim. The carousel whirled and displayed a seemingly endless supply of suitcases and bags for the travelers.

Lauren Cooper stood on the other side of the carousel and pointedly avoided looking at him. She looked small and alone in the press of people around her. Most everyone else in the crowd was paired up or part of a larger group. Overall, she appeared vulnerable, like the way he remembered her from the day they'd met in the morgue.

"What is she doing there?" Jackson Portman sounded as irritated as Heath felt.

"She's not down here for the sand and surf."

"You want to know what I think?"

"No." Heath scanned the baggage for his suitcase.

"I'm gonna tell you anyway. I think things are crazy enough with you down there on your own. With Lauren Cooper there, too? Things are just gonna get crazier. That's what I think."

"Maybe while you've got your head clear from all that thinking you can find out where she's going to be staying down here."

"How am I supposed to do that?"

"Call her mother. Tell her you're following up on some leads about her daughter's murder and that an investigator needs to talk to Lauren."

"You want me to lie to her mother?"

"Yes."

"See, now this is when you carry this whole partnership thing too far. You don't lie to mothers, man. They know stuff. Part of the stuff they know is when you're lying. Santa Claus powers ain't got nothing on mother powers."

"I know stuff, too. If I don't keep an eye on Lauren Cooper, she's going to end up in a lot of trouble. And since I'm going to be watching Gibson, too, my life would be simpler if I knew where she was staying." Heath reached down for his suitcase, caught the handle and took it from the treadmill. "Don't make me do all the heavy lifting."

"Couldn't you just follow her? You being a detective and all?"

"I'm going to. Call the mother. Get back to me." With his suitcase in one hand, Heath headed for the outer perimeter of the crowd. He glanced over his shoulder and saw that Lauren had a skycap handling her bags. *Bags.* Evidently she was planning on staying for a while.

Heath's gut clenched at the thought of the danger she was going to be in. She wasn't thinking straight. She'd just lost her sister. And she wasn't trained for anything like this.

She hadn't seen him yet, so he headed straight for the exit doors, intending to get a cab so he could follow her. He could return later to pick up the rental he'd arranged. He stood in line waiting.

A moment later, Lauren walked through the doors with her luggage in tow. And she walked directly to a waiting private car. Realizing she had arranged for the pickup at the airport ahead of time, that she was about to get away, Heath tried to get through the crowd.

Unable to reach the car in time, Heath stepped out in front of the vehicle as it drove away. The driver barely acknowledged him and might even have run him down had he not stepped back. Frustrated and feeling a little panicked, almost the way he'd felt when he'd driven to the hospital after he'd been told Janet had been admitted, he watched helplessly as Lauren Cooper vanished.

Chapter 7

Baking in the midday tropical heat, relishing the cool breeze that streamed in from the ocean, Heath tried in vain to find a comfortable position in his rental car. After hours spent seated there, though, comfort seemed to be impossible. He'd parked near the public beach close to Gibson's villa.

A stone wall ran around the perimeter of the estate, marking off a large chunk of private landscape filled with palm trees that stood up like a child's pinwheels, bougainvillea and other flowers that Heath couldn't identify. Although the stone wall was at least three hundred years old, maybe older, it was covered with the latest in high-tech security. There was also on-site security with at least nine guards that worked in rotation. Heath had figured that out on his previous visit and reconfirmed that during the two days since his return.

Between Heath's vantage point under a copse of palm trees and the mansion three hundred yards away, people lounged on the beach. Most of them were tourists, pale skin showing pink from the sun. But there were a few fishermen on a short wooden pier who seemed more interested in telling stories and drinking beer than in catching anything. In the middle, a spirited volleyball game took place between what looked like college-age guys and girls. They called out encouragement and derision to each other, and that was punctuated by sharp barks of laughter. Out on the water, a few small sailboats with brightly colored sails glided toward the horizon.

Heath pulled at his shirt to allow a breeze in, then cleaned his sunglasses to get the sweat streaks off the lenses. He pushed the sunglasses up again and picked up the binoculars lying on the passenger seat. He trained the binocs on the mansion.

C'mon, do something. You can't just want to sit

in that house all day and all night. Heath raked the house from side to side and top to bottom, searching in vain for Gibson. For the past two days and both nights, there had been no activity at the villa. Nobody went in and nobody went out. Heath still didn't know Gibson's schedule. Inside the house, the man was invisible and un-knowable.

Frustrated, Heath started to put the binocs away, but a familiar figure caught his eye. He adjusted the magnification and brought in the woman lounging on a chaise on the outer edge of the volleyball game. He wasn't sure what had caught his attention, maybe the set of her jaw, maybe her hair or maybe the fact that she was watching Gibson's villa with the same intensity he was.

But he knew her in a heartbeat. Lauren Cooper sat in the chair wearing a white bikini that set off a figure that had more curves than Heath would have guessed. Her skin looked smooth and satiny, with just enough of a tan to blunt the sun's harsh rays. She wore her hair pulled back under a floppy hat. Large sunglasses obscured the top part of her face, but he knew it was her. Her tablet lay on her taut stomach.

Unable to stop himself, Heath drank in every inch of her, for a moment forgetting the White Rabbit murders, Janet and his frustration at being unable to break the case. Lauren Cooper was beautiful, and lying there she looked even more vulnerable than he'd thought she was.

During the past two days, her whereabouts in Kingston had remained a mystery. Jackson Portman's conversation with the mother hadn't gone well. The woman hadn't known where Lauren was, and she'd been surprised that her daughter wasn't at home or at work, so Jackson had only succeeded in agitating her.

Since his return to Kingston, Heath had set up surveillance on Gibson. He'd expected to spot her somewhere along the way because he knew she wouldn't be able to stay away from the magician. But he hadn't seen her, and he had begun to worry that something had already happened to her. Even though seeing her there irritated him, he felt relieved at the same time.

Lauren reached down for a bottle of water she kept by the chaise and sipped the contents through a straw. Heath relished the smooth play of toned muscle under her skin as she shifted in the chair.

At least she wasn't trying to bum rush the front gates. On the first day of surveillance, Heath had halfway expected her to do that. When he'd thought of that, he hadn't known what to fear more—her alerting Gibson or getting accepted inside.

Lauren got up without warning and dropped her tablet into the big beach bag beside the chaise. She folded the chair, grabbed her bag, and headed toward a small parking lot a short distance away.

Caught up in the undulation of her hips, Heath took a moment to realize what had gotten Lauren up and moving. He switched the binocs back to the villa just in time to see the wrought-iron gates part and a sleek black Jaguar sedan patiently waiting like a predator. Once the gates were open, the luxury car slid through like a bullet.

Heath scanned the car as he reached for his keys and started his rental. The engine turned over smoothly and caught. The vents blew hot air into the side of his face.

The Jaguar's windows were tinted so dark they looked like sheets of oil. Heath caught only a glimpse of the driver, a powerful-looking man named Deke Roylston. Roylston was a hard case who was no stranger to breaking the law, but his record was spotty over the years. The man had worked as a mercenary in his younger days before settling in as Gibson's bodyguard six years ago.

Nothing in the paper trail connected Roylston, but he worked for a professional security service based in Seattle, Washington, and had been on permanent assignment in Kingston for the past six years. Poking into the security company's background hadn't been easy, and Heath hadn't learned much. They were a high-end executive protective service used to providing bodyguards to corporate personnel and celebrities.

Heath put the transmission in drive and wheeled his vehicle around, taking up the pursuit back to Kingston. As he drove, he adjusted the .357 Magnum partially concealed under his right thigh. Thankfully, there was some tourist traffic on the road. He was able to tuck in a couple of cars behind the Jaguar. When he glanced in the rearview mirror, he caught a glimpse of Lauren behind the wheel of a nondescript white compact rental as she slid behind a car behind him.

Then she was gone from sight, but Heath could still feel her back there. He snarled a curse. *Get your head back in the game. One thing at a time. Focus on your guy. Take him out and everybody's safe.*

That was what he had been doing when Janet had been killed, though.

Trance music played over the Jaguar's sound system, filling the rear seat with techno sounds and synth. The female singer's voice sent chills rippling down Gibson's back.

Gibson steepled his hands in front of him and stared through the windshield at the sun-blasted road ahead of them. "Is he back there?"

Even though Gibson was sure Roylston already knew the police officer was tailing them, the big man checked the rearview mirror anyway. "Yes."

Gibson smiled and felt satisfied. "Good." The

acknowledgment was double-edged, intended more to irritate Roylston than to respond in polite fashion.

"Out here, you're vulnerable." Roylston looked back in the rearview mirror, locking eyes briefly with Gibson. "There's just me. You'd be safer back at the villa."

"Others will be waiting at the restaurant."

"There's miles to go between here and there."

"Lighten up, Deke. You should be enjoying this. A game of cat and mouse like this? You should be eating it up. When you stopped killing people for pay to protect me, some part of you must surely miss the excitement."

"No."

"Not even a smidgen?"

"You haven't been in that position, being out in the jungle, not knowing when the next step is gonna be on a mine, or if a sniper has you in his sights from a thousand yards away. That's not fun. That's hell."

"You could have chosen another career."

"The pay was good."

"Not that good. You enjoyed what you did.

And you enjoy what you're doing now. You enjoy being around me."

"You cause too much trouble."

"For which you're paid quite handsomely. Never forget that. And never forget that I've looked into your files. You were no saint. You took your pound of flesh and your pleasure where and when you wanted to while you were over there. Maybe you've even done that here."

Roylston didn't reply.

Gibson put his arm on the rests and drummed his fingers in time to the music. He stretched his legs out, enjoying the little pulse of adrenaline singing through his blood.

Roylston drove on in silence for a time, but he couldn't keep his thoughts to himself. Gibson knew the man was going to break his silence by the way he held his shoulders. That was another game just the two of them played.

"You're pushing this cop too far."

Gibson folded his arms behind his head and radiated the perfect picture of indolence. "Do you think so?"

"Yeah, I do. You shouldn't have killed his partner."

Gibson smiled. "Maybe you shouldn't have let me. As I recall, that happened on your watch."

Roylston grimaced and his voice thickened. "Maybe you're pushing *me* too far, too."

"Really?" Gibson feigned surprise.

Roylston started to say something, then closed his mouth and focused on the road.

"Do you ever wonder why you got saddled with me?"

Roylston made no reply.

"I think it's because you had some indiscretions of your own. I think you were assigned to me to do penance for philandering with my father's ex-fiancée. A good security man should know better, shouldn't he?"

Roylston glared at him in the mirror.

"You pretend you have a moral compass, but you don't. Not really. Everybody is out to get what they think they want. Whatever captures their attention, whatever new thing they think their heart desires. Most of them end up unhappy and they don't even know why."

"Killing those women makes you happy?"

This time Gibson's smile was real. Excitement flared through him because he knew he'd penetrated the bodyguard more than he ever had before. "Yes, actually it does. I love knowing their lives are mine to do with as I please. That I have that much control over someone else. And I know that you know what I'm talking about. You've been there, too. But that's not the best part."

"Then what is?"

Gibson rolled the coin across his knuckles. "What makes me happy is making my father unhappy. I kill those women because I know he fears me getting caught and embarrassing him. So I kill the women and you people have to clean up the mess. When you can find the victims, which you haven't always been able to do. That's the game I play with my father. He chose you to watch over me because he doesn't care for you after the philandering incident. Working with me is your penance, but you'll never be able to pay that off. My father doesn't let people out from under his thumb. You have to make your own way out from under."

Roylston drove on for a short time in silence. The outskirts of Kingston were just ahead, buildings suddenly filling the empty expanse of jungle and beach. Hotels and business centers in the New Kingston area looked white and stark against the blue sky.

"Your old man's gonna get tired of playing games with you one of these days."

"Do you think so?" Gibson relished toying with the man.

"I would."

"You're not my father. To him, I'm irreplace-able."

"Seems to me he replaced your mother pretty quick when the time came."

Anger burned bright and ember hot, and Gibson felt the heat rising to his face. The coin disappeared from his hands, and the .45 ACP Derringer pistol he carried appeared as he leaned forward. He pushed the barrel against the base of Roylston's skull.

"Don't talk about my mother. *Ever.*" His voice was a cold growl, breath that blew over a wood rasp.

"Pull that trigger and we both die."

"No. If I pull this trigger, you die. *Maybe* I'll die." Then Gibson laughed, palmed the pistol again, made a fist, then slowly opened it to show that it was empty as Roylston watched him in the rearview mirror. "I could take my chances with the car's safety features." He leaned back in the plush seat. "Or I can just wait till you're asleep some night in your room, step in and blow your brains out." Smiling, he laced his fingers behind his head. "Your successor can clean up the mess."

Roylston shifted uncomfortably in the seat. He cleared his throat, but he didn't say anything.

"Let me worry about Detective Heath Sawyer." Lackadaisically, Gibson gazed through the side window out at the approaching line of the metro area. "You just sit back and enjoy the show."

Chapter 8

Oyster Rose Restaurant catered to the afflu-
ent tourist class. It occupied an old, converted
warehouse three blocks back of the ocean, but
the second-floor veranda offered a good view
of the coastline and the sunsets over the city.
The original architecture had been kept for the
most part, but a lot of work had gone into the
interior.

Heath had heard of the restaurant since he'd
been in Kingston, but he couldn't remember
where he'd first learned about it. The business
was one of the high-traffic destinations for tourists, and it was expensive and hard to get reservations for. A couple dozen people sat in the
waiting area to one side of the building. Servers

brought out drinks, ensuring that guests would run up a profitable tab before they ever got a table.

After Gibson had arrived at the restaurant, Heath had parked in a lot across the street from the lot where the driver had left Gibson's car. Then he'd followed at a safe distance. Neither the driver nor Gibson paid him any attention, and he thought they were unaware of him. There were enough people in the restaurant even in the afternoon that Heath felt certain he could blend in while escaping notice.

Gibson was either a regular at the restaurant, or the owners were fans or he had a reservation. As soon as he arrived, one of the hostesses wearing a shimmery flowered dress that clung just enough to hint at the curves lying beneath went to him and guided him to a table with a good view of the harbor.

Laughing and joking with the hostess, Gibson took the offered seat. Roylston sat opposite him. The table was positioned just far enough away to discourage conversation with other guests. A few of them recognized the magician or at least thought they did. Heath could tell that from the body language of the guests as they leaned in to talk quietly among themselves.

Gibson ignored them and contented himself with the iPad he'd brought with him. He made no attempt to talk to Roylston. The bodyguard sat languidly in his chair, but his eyes roved over the other diners, and his jacket, tailored to disguise the pistol Heath was certain was holstered under his right arm, was left loose.

A stool opened up at the end of the bar. Heath stepped up and took the seat, still able to watch Gibson's table.

"Hi. What can I get you?" The female bartender on the other side of the bar was petite and had her hair up in dreadlocks.

"Beer. Bottled. Domestic is fine." Heath took money from his pants pocket and paid her when she handed him the beer dripping ice water. The bartender went away as Heath sipped his beer. The ice-cold beer hit the back of his throat and felt like heaven. He ran the chilled bottle across his forehead.

Televisions hanging in different areas of the restaurant broadcasted baseball and soccer games. Other televisions offered continuous advertisements of activities and scenery around the island.

Heath watched Gibson, but he kept an eye out for Lauren, as well. He'd seen her car a couple of times on the way into Kingston and he didn't think she'd gotten lost. Of course, it was possible. He was also afraid that something had happened to her, that maybe Gibson coming into Kingston was just a feint to draw her out so that some of his bodyguards could seize her.

You're seeing conspiracies everywhere. Stop. Take a breath. It's entirely possible that she got lost. Heath sipped more of his beer.

A server brought drinks to Gibson's table. A mixed drink for Gibson and coffee for Roylston. Gibson continued to be amused by whatever he was looking at on his iPad.

Heath hated the way Gibson grinned at whatever he was checking out on the device. He thought of how he'd seen Janet, of how he hadn't been there when she'd needed him. And he thought about how Lauren Cooper had looked down in the morgue when she'd gone to identify her sister.

Nobody should have to hurt like that.

And the guy who was responsible for that pain shouldn't get to enjoy his life.

That wasn't going to happen.

Before he knew he was moving, Heath pushed away from the bar and threaded through the tables with single-minded focus. He was barely aware of bumping into people, but he didn't care.

Roylston noticed Heath's laser-beam approach immediately. The big man stood and crossed his arms over his broad chest, putting himself out there as a human roadblock between Heath and Gibson.

Gibson gave no indication that he'd even noticed the bodyguard's movement.

"All right." The bodyguard's voice was gruff and low, just threatening enough to be a vocal speed bump. "That's far enough. You take another step and you're going to get hurt."

Anger stirred inside Heath. He wasn't worried about getting hurt. In fact, getting hurt might even feel good. When his temper flared back as he was playing sports, it felt good to hit and to get hit.

Heath kept coming, stepping into the bodyguard. Roylston put his hand on Heath's chest to stop him. Lifting his left arm, Heath batted the man's hand away and took another step.

At the same time, two large men at tables on either side of Gibson stood and reached to their hips. Their jackets kept the weapons concealed, but Heath knew immediately they were carrying.

"Detective Sawyer." Gibson's voice was cool and crisp. He lifted his gaze from the iPad, pushed the device onto the table, and steepled his fingers as he rested his elbows there. He smirked, and his dark eyes glowed with magnetic intensity.

Heath made himself breathe and work through his anger. He still wanted to smash Roylston down, if that was possible, and go for Gibson. But that wasn't how he was going to make his case. All he wanted to do here was rattle Gibson's cage, shake the man up and let him know that not everyone was just going to walk away from what he'd done.

"What can I do for you?" Gibson sipped his drink and leaned back in his seat.

"I just wanted you to know that I haven't gone away, that I was still here turning over rocks."

Gibson leaned back in his seat, totally at ease. "Should I feel threatened? Be impressed by your single-minded intent? Maybe even be proud of your stubborn insistence?" He grinned. "What do you want from me?"

Heath grinned back, a thin, mirthless expression tight on his face and feeling as if it had been frozen there. "I just want the truth about those murders."

Gibson sipped his drink again. "Careful, Detective. You're in a public place. You're coming awfully close to slander."

Nearly all the afternoon crowd had paused their lunches to observe what was taking place. A few families had left their tables and were edging toward the door.

Heath felt bad about that, but he couldn't stop himself. He was barely able to control the white-hot fury that threatened to explode from him. That night of horror, trying to deal with Janet's husband and kids, was indelibly marked in his mind. And thinking about how Lauren Cooper seemed to be determined to involve herself with Gibson pushed him past the point of no return. He didn't want her to get hurt.

"No slander here, but I'll make you a promise." Heath's voice was stronger and colder and harder than he would have believed. "You're not going to get away with what you've done."

"Hollow words, Detective." Gibson took in an easy breath. "You can't prove I've gotten away with anything."

"I will."

A little round man wearing a suit and a frown walked to Heath's side. "Please, sir, I must ask that you leave the premises. Otherwise I will be forced to summon the police. I am sure neither one of us wants that."

Heath didn't want that. He didn't know how much it would take to get him thrown out of the city, but he definitely wanted to stop short of that point. If Lauren was going to insanely continue her observation of Gibson, Heath wanted to pull all of the man's attention to himself and hope that the woman escaped notice.

"Sure. I'll go." Heath locked eyes with Gibson, but the magician just returned his attention to his iPad. "But I'll be around."

A gold coin suddenly appeared in Gibson's

hand, then rolled across his knuckles and disappeared in a twinkling.

Seething, barely under control, Heath turned and left the restaurant. Roylston and his two companions didn't return to their seats till after Heath had stepped into the street and headed for the parking lot. Two of the restaurant staff followed him, both of them good-sized guys who probably handled aggressive guests.

Heath swore at himself. He had intended to play the surveillance cool. Just watch and learn. But thinking of Lauren Cooper getting involved and perhaps getting hurt because she didn't know any better had thrown him off his game. The woman was going to cause all sorts of problems for—

From the corner of his eye, Heath caught sight of a familiar figure walking into the restaurant.

Lauren had ditched the beachwear for a lightweight dress that accentuated her figure. Heath realized that the only way she could have possibly gotten dressed that quickly around here was changing in the car on the drive over. He hadn't been at the restaurant that long. Imagining her changing her clothing in the car was distracting, and by the time he'd realized she was still moving, she was inside the restaurant.

Heath tried to follow, but two staff members stepped toward him. The bigger one shook his head.

Disgusted with the situation, Heath held up his hands in surrender, then turned and jogged across the street to his car. He unlocked the door and climbed inside, then picked up his binoculars and followed Lauren Cooper's progress through the restaurant.

She looked beautiful...and too vulnerable.

Walking through the restaurant was a performance. Lauren focused on that, telling herself that again and again as she closed in on Gibson's table. She didn't take a direct route because that would have drawn too much attention and possibly put the man on the defensive. She wasn't sure exactly how she wanted to approach Gibson, but she thought if she could get him talking, maybe she could learn something.

She paused at the bar long enough to order a glass of wine. From her vantage point, she had a clear view of Gibson. The man seemed consumed by his tablet, pausing every now and again to tap on the surface, presumably sending emails.

He didn't look like a killer. Lauren had tried to picture Gibson as that, as the man who had taken Megan's life, but she couldn't. The man was magic, capable of captivating an audience and doing the impossible right before everyone's eyes. The magicians who gathered at the magic store spoke of Gibson with awe and envy. Many of them didn't understand how Gibson had hit the public eye so easily. His connections with the media had seemed equally as magical.

She sipped her wine, barely tasting it.

Screwing up her courage, afraid that Gibson was only there for drinks and would soon get up and leave, Lauren left the wine on the bar and headed in the general direction of the bathroom.

On the way there, Gibson pierced her with his stare.

For a moment, Lauren was afraid that Gibson had somehow recognized her. Megan had carried photos of them together in her purse. If Gibson had killed Megan, he might have gone through her things. There was nothing in the

White Rabbit files that had indicated any such interest, though. The man had simply killed his victims. Except for Detective Janet Hutchins. The killer had taken his time and tortured her.

This is a performance. Perform. Lauren forced herself to smile and turned to face Gibson. She turned off all her feelings of loss and pain and battened them down deep inside herself the way she had when she'd been in the foster homes. She'd learned how to perform there first, and she'd learned how to be invisible even in a crowd.

She crossed the distance to Gibson's table and held out a hand, holding her clasp purse in her other hand. "Gibson? *The* Gibson? The magician?" She put as much "ooh" and "ahh" into her voice as she could, surprised at how easy it was even under these conditions. She was a fan of his work, after all.

The man seated at the table stood and put a hand out to block her advance, stopping just short of actually touching her. "I'm going to have to ask you to stand back, miss."

"I'm sorry. I just couldn't help myself." Lauren continued to look at Gibson. "It's just that I'm one of your biggest fans. I saw the show you did in—" she started to say Chicago, then realized that might remind him of Megan and make him cautious "—Minneapolis two years ago." She had seen the Chicago show in person, with Megan, but she had watched the Minneapolis performance on HBO. "I still can't figure out how you made that big Humvee disappear."

Gibson plucked a speared olive from his drink and leaned back in his seat. He popped the olive into his mouth and bit down. "It was magic, of course."

Lauren forced herself to grin like a loon. "Of course it was." She looked at the table. "I'm sorry. I didn't mean to interrupt your lunch."

The big man took his hand back but didn't sit. He kept his face neutral and never took his gaze from her. "Mr. Gibson prefers his space."

"I understand. I don't mean to be a bother, but I didn't know you were here. Are you performing?"

Gibson shook his head and flashed white teeth. "No. A bit of a vacation actually."

Lauren smiled. "This is a great place for a vacation." Several of the nearby guests kept track of the conversation with obvious interest.

Gibson's gaze traveled up and down Lauren, and for a moment the cold appraisal in his dark eyes made her want to shiver. Part of his interest was sexual, she recognized that, and she squelched her immediate impulse to walk away. There was something dirty and hungry in Gibson's attention, and that surprised her.

This man killed Megan. The thought rocketed through Lauren's head with iron-clad conviction. She didn't know precisely what had caused her to suddenly believe that, but she did.

"It is." Gibson dropped the plastic spear from the olive back into his empty drink glass. "You should enjoy your time here. Now, if you'll excuse me, I think that's my lunch." He pointed over her shoulder.

Turning slightly, Lauren found one of the servers waiting patiently behind her with food on a tray. Lauren stepped back out of the way. "I apologize for coming over."

Gibson ignored her, focusing on the server as she placed the salad, soup and seafood dish on the table in front of him. "Not a problem. I'm glad you enjoyed the show. I look forward to bedazzling you in the future."

Dismissed, Lauren started to go. She had never in her life tried to approach a man like that, hoping to get herself invited to his table. Getting sent on her way in such a cavalier fashion actually stung in spite of all the other mixed feelings about Megan. It also frustrated her because she didn't know how she was supposed to get close enough to the man to find out more.

"Miss."

Lauren turned back to Gibson. He held up an empty hand, then turned it, closed it and opened it again. A silver coin lay in his palm.

"A memento, perhaps?" Gibson held the coin perched at the end of his thumb and forefinger.

"I'd love one." Lauren made herself smile as she reached for the coin. The metal felt cold and hard against her skin. She closed it in her fist. "Thank you. I'll be looking forward to your next show."

Gibson nodded, but his attention was already on the meal in front of him.

Lauren headed back to the bathroom feeling miserable but turned and walked out of the restaurant a different way than she'd entered. She felt miserable because seeing Gibson there, so nonchalantly going on with his life even if he hadn't killed Megan—which Lauren no longer believed—bothered her deeply. She wasn't going to just walk away and accept things, but she didn't know what she was going to do to change things, either.

A large shadow fell over Lauren as she used the key fob to open the locks on her rental. She checked the reflection in the window glass to see who had made the shadow. She thought it might be the big man who had been sitting with Gibson. That guy had looked as if he was no stranger to violence.

She turned around with the keys clenched between her fingers, ready to strike out if she had to. Her other hand held her clasp purse, but her fingers had already started lifting the door handle.

Heath Sawyer stopped only a few inches away, just short of touching her. The heat from his body radiated against her, and the smell of his cologne and natural musk filled her nose and made her senses dance. God, why did the man have to look so good? She had never been so captivated by a man she'd spent so little time with.

Part of that was blunted by the angry set to his mouth and jaw. His sunglasses hid his eyes. When he spoke, his voice came out as a half growl.

"What do you think you were doing in there?"

"I was trying to prove you wrong about Gibson. I thought if I talked to him, maybe I could find out something that you and the local police haven't been able to discover about Megan's death." Anger poured out of Lauren and she directed it at Heath. "You were so sure of yourself that I thought you were too locked in to know what you were doing."

"He's the guy who killed your sister."

Lauren took a breath. "I know."

Heath had started to say something. Now he paused, thought for a moment, and closed his mouth. The blank lenses over his eyes hid any clue as to what he was thinking. "You know he's the guy? Did he say something to you?"

"Like, 'I did it? I killed your sister, and I killed all those other women'?" Lauren shook her head and crossed her arms. She was on the verge of tears, and she didn't like that. Crying was a weakness. It didn't solve any problems, and often it only made them worse. If she could have gotten in her car and driven away, she would have been all right. Heath Sawyer had just caught her at the wrong time. "No, he didn't say anything like that."

"Then what did he say?"

"He gave me this." Lauren handed over the coin she'd gotten from Gibson. It was a two-headed disc that featured Gibson on stage on one side and an empty stage on the other.

Heath took the coin and looked at it. "What's this?"

"One of Gibson's tokens. He uses them in his magic act in front of audiences. Hands them out so people can flash them around, tell everybody they've seen the amazing Gibson." Lauren heard the vitriol in her words and was surprised. Only a short time ago she'd been a Gibson fan intending to prove the magician's innocence.

"He gave this to you?"

"Yes."

"Why?"

"Because he's a jerk. Because he thought I

was his Number One Fan and this was consolation prize because I didn't get to talk with him more." With deceptive ease, Lauren plucked the coin from Heath's fingers, then rolled it across her knuckles, exposing the sides in rapid syncopation. "See how Gibson seems to appear and disappear? It's an optical illusion if you learn how to roll the coin right."

She popped the coin into the air so that it spun and caught the bright sunlight. Then she caught it in her palm, closed her hand and turned it over, palmed it smoothly with her other hand while she acted like she was pointing to her hand with her forefinger. When she opened her hand, the coin was gone.

Stone-faced, Heath looked at her. She was suddenly aware of how close they were, and it was almost like he was giving off enough gravity to pull her into his orbit. For a moment, she wanted to just lean in and give herself over to him, let him put his arms around her and tell her everything was going to be all right. She wanted comfort from him like she hadn't wanted anything in a long time.

Instead, Heath remained those few inches away.

"You need to stay out of this. You don't know what you're doing. You don't know how much danger you're exposing yourself to."

That rekindled the anger inside Lauren, and she gave herself over to it. "You don't get to tell me what to do."

"Believe me, it's not a privilege. You're interfering with police business."

"What police business?" Her voice came out louder than she'd expected and drew the attention of a small group of passersby. "This isn't your turf, Detective Sawyer. You don't have any more right here than I do, and you definitely don't have the right to tell me what I can and can't do."

"Somebody needs to. You're out of control."

"Out of control?" Lauren clamped her jaw on a torrent of swear words only because some of the people walking past had small children in their care. She lowered her voice with effort. "I'm not out of control."

"Yeah, you are." Heath cocked his head to one side. "You should be home, not here."

"What would I do there?"

"Grieve. Go back to work. Take care of your

mother. From what I saw at the funeral, she needs someone there with her right now."

The sudden guilt felt like salt rubbed into a wound. "Leave my mother out of this."

His face softened a little and his voice gentled. "You can do more good there than you can here."

Lauren knew the argument was a good one, and that it was probably true, but she also knew she couldn't walk away from the investigation into Gibson. Maybe Megan would have gone with the magician anyway that night, because he was a good-looking man, but she'd been made more vulnerable by Lauren's interest in him. She couldn't leave while Gibson was loose. She didn't like feeling helpless, and she didn't appreciate Heath pointing that out. "Like you're doing so much good here. Why don't you go home and grieve over your partner? Maybe that's what you should be doing."

Too late, Lauren knew that what she'd said was too much. It was more than she'd intended, just spewed out of painful vindictiveness. Despite the sunglasses, the hurt showed on Heath's face. She wanted to apologize, but she didn't know how to start and was convinced that, at the moment at least, any apology would do no good.

His voice turned cold and hard. "If you keep interfering with Gibson, you're going to get yourself hurt."

Lauren couldn't back off. She wasn't going to be cowed or sent to her room like that little girl she'd been. She'd come a long way since those days. "Maybe if I do, you'll catch him this time."

Heath snarled inarticulately and turned away from her. He never looked back as he crossed the street to another parking lot.

Lauren got into the hot car, turned the engine on and set the air-conditioner on high. *Great trick there, Lauren. Alienate the only guy who might be able to help you.* She leaned her head on the steering wheel for a moment, then she centered herself, put the car in gear and headed back to her hotel. She didn't know where else to go at the moment.

Chapter 9

The next two days passed like vague memories of the first. Lauren set up on the beach with a view of Gibson's villa and kept watch. The magician stayed put. A few of his men went into the city, always in pairs. On the second day, Lauren followed them and discovered they were evidently taking downtime away from the villa, visiting restaurants and strip clubs. The Palais Royale Night Club seemed to be the favorite.

During that excursion, Lauren noted that Heath had evidently had the same idea or had followed her. He always positioned himself where he could watch over her and the villa, and that irritated her because it meant he didn't trust her to keep herself safe.

When the two bodyguards went into a club called the Bronze Parrot, Heath followed. The reggae beat swirled out over the street as hucksters in front of the bar shouted out to passing pedestrian traffic and cars.

The thought of Heath watching dancers gyrate inside the club bothered Lauren more than she wanted it to. He was just there observing the two bodyguards. She knew that, but the idea of him inside the club chafed her.

She briefly considered following him into the club, then put it out of her mind. Her beachwear wasn't appropriate attire for the place, and she had nothing suitable to wear into the club in the back of the car. In fact, she hoped she had nothing suitable to wear there at all.

She turned the car around and retreated to the villa, telling herself that she was going to catch Gibson leaving, and Heath would miss out.

That didn't happen. She spent the day watching the villa, and nothing stirred. Hours later, Heath followed the bodyguards back and resumed his observation post.

As she sat in the chaise and listened to the sound of the gentle waves lapping at the coastline and the laughing voices of the volleyball players, Lauren used her iPhone to access Twitter. She'd keyed in Gibson's name as a trending topic. Unfortunately, since *Gibson* was the only name she was able to enter and *Gibson Magician* didn't pull up Tweets any better, she had to sort through a lot of entries.

Shortly before sundown, she received an email from Morganstern.

Lauren,

I've just heard from Sinclair that Gibson will be at a nightclub called the Bright Blue Calypso tonight. Sinclair's cousin is a travel agent who handles reservations for Gibson's agent, Devon Walters. The information should be good.

I hope that you are well. We are doing fine here, and I must say that being back in the store is exciting. I've seen a couple of illusions that I think are going to astonish audiences when they're revealed. I can't wait to show them to you on your return. And I must say that you should come home soon. Viv and I worry about you.

Your mother is fine. I've been to check on her myself. She is concerned about you down there,

but I'm sure you've already heard from her regarding that.

Be safe and come home soon.

The Amazing Morganstern J

Lauren smiled at the email and quickly dashed
off a reply, thanking him for the information and
reassuring him that she was quite all right, just
still not ready to come home.

As she was finishing that off, an email from
her mother arrived. The email was short and to
the point, talking briefly about her recent visit
to the doctor and how everything still looked
hopeful, and that she missed her and wished she
would come back home, though she understood
the need to do something.

If I weren't laid up with chemo, I would be
there with you. I think I've read far more detective novels than you have. LOL

The attempt at humor brought a tear to Lauren's eye. She wiped it away as the cool, salt
breeze ran across her and made her realize how
late it was getting. She emailed her mom to let

her know she was fine, then closed down the email app on her phone and glanced back at the villa. Lights glowed in some of the windows.

The problem was getting to Gibson. The bodyguards kept the man too closely supervised. They were like stage assistants, visible and invisible as needed, but the focus remained on Gibson.

Realizing that gave Lauren another idea. Maybe she couldn't separate Gibson from his bodyguards, but she might be able to separate one of the bodyguards from their employer. And she thought she knew how to do it.

She was going to need help, though.

Getting to her feet, she folded the chaise and carried it and her water bottle to her rental, stashing everything in the trunk. Then she walked back toward Heath Sawyer's car.

Heath noted Lauren's approach at once and appreciated the smooth roll of toned flesh as she made her way to him. His heart felt firmly lodged in the back of his throat as he noted the swell of her breasts and the cleavage captured by the yellow-and-orange swirled string bikini she wore today.

He'd watched her earlier, and he'd ended up paying far too much attention to her. That was part of the reason he'd decided to tail Gibson's bodyguards into Kingston earlier that day. The other part was because he knew she would watch Gibson. Eventually whatever she learned, he would know. Whether they liked it or not, they were working together.

She wore her dark hair swept in an updo that left her neck long and beautiful…and too vulnerable. Heath couldn't get the memory of the bruises around her sister's neck from his mind. She'd pushed her yellow sunglasses up into her hair, and the look totally worked for her, even though he was certain she hadn't consciously chosen to make a look. She only wore mascara and eyeliner. Her skin glowed from being in the sun all day.

He didn't let his guard down, though.

She came to a stop a yard away and crossed her arms. "Gibson's supposed to go out tonight."

That irritated Heath. She wasn't supposed to be better informed than he was. "You're sure?"

"Yes. He has a reservation at Bright Blue Calypso tonight."

"What's that?"

"A nightclub." She gave him the address as he reached for a pad lying in the passenger seat next to the binocs.

He finished writing the address and looked up at her. "Why are you telling me?"

"I thought maybe we could work together."

Heath was shaking his head before she finished. "No. Not a chance. There is no *we*."

She shrugged. "All right." She turned around and walked away.

"You need to stay away from there."

Lauren tossed him a wave over her shoulder but never missed a step.

He watched her go, mesmerized by the way her hips twitched, thinking that he wished that she wasn't so hardheaded.

The Bright Blue Calypso Club featured soul-driven calypso music, which was no shock, but the elegance of the club surprised Lauren. It was located on the bottom floor of one of the downtown office buildings and existed within its own bubble.

The crowd was wild and fun, and the dance floor stayed packed. Bright blue lasers shifted and danced through the darkness filling the upper reaches of the high ceiling. The sound system rocked the house and the music was live from a colorfully dressed band on a well-lit stage.

Sitting at a small table against one wall in the club, Lauren sipped her beer and watched the front door. It was 8:17, probably still early for Gibson. The table that had been reserved for him still sat empty in front of the band.

Lauren didn't think Gibson would be there just for the music, so she puzzled over what would bring him to the club. She wore a strappy mini black cocktail dress that hit her at midthigh and black heels, and wore black bangles on her right wrist. The bangles looked like polished ebony and caught the light when she moved. They were a distraction she planned to use. She kept her hair moussed back. thinking that she looked a lot different than she had when she'd confronted Gibson in the restaurant.

Her stomach fluttered nervously as she considered what she was about to do. She'd never done anything like this, and what she was prepared to do could easily land her in jail.

You'll do fine. Easy-peasy. You've worked an audience before, and this isn't much different.

Except that what she planned on doing was illegal. Failure or success, she was going to be in a lot of trouble if she got caught.

The fact that Heath Sawyer hadn't yet shown up further unnerved her. He had seemed liked the reliable type, and she got frustrated with herself for thinking that—for *counting* on that— when it was evidently not true.

She sipped her beer and watched the door.

At 8:32, Gibson strolled through the front door with his primary bodyguard. The big man came ahead of Gibson and scanned the premises, one hand resting lightly under the fold of his coat.

As usual, Gibson was dressed all in black, wearing a black leather jacket over his turtleneck. His hair was neatly combed, and he looked like a lord who had stepped into a night out with the provincials. A small smile played on his full lips for a moment, then he was distracted as a small feminine figure wriggled up under his arm.

Lauren's heart sped up and fear turned cold inside her as she studied the young woman.

She was in her early twenties, if that, and looked as if Gibson had cut her out from one of the college groups vacationing in the city. She had chestnut-colored hair that had been teased into wild abandon, a shocking pink mini-dress with a broad black belt and a figure meant to be sheathed in it. She gazed around the club with wide-eyed innocence, but she carried a smart-phone in her right hand, and she was already photographing the sights.

Lauren looked at the young woman. She wanted to go over to her and tell her to get away from Gibson, but she didn't know if that would do any good. More than likely, it wouldn't. She pushed aside the fear for the girl. If everything she had planned worked out, Gibson wouldn't be taking anyone home anyway.

One of the cocktail servers met Gibson and his party and led them over to the reserved table. The girl squealed in delight and hugged Gibson fiercely. Her pink nails flashed across her smartphone and Lauren felt certain that Tweets were going up by the dozen. Maybe that alone would be enough to prevent her from ending up another victim.

Gibson sat at the table with his primary body-guard. Two others took up positions nearby. Both of them were middle-aged, hard-bodied and alert, but one of them had an eye for the women. His hair was moussed back, and he had an arrogant body language. He was good-look-ing and he knew it, and that attitude was already drawing women to him.

Lauren chose him as her mark. She finished her beer, took the empty bottle and placed it onto the tray of a passing server, and walked toward the bodyguard. As she swept the dance crowd, she spotted Heath Sawyer on the other side of the room. He was dressed in a casual sports jacket, slacks and a pullover that allowed him to effort-lessly fit into the younger crowd. She was sur-prised at how much he had changed.

Evidently her appearance caught him off guard as well, because he had to look twice to recog-nize her. She knew he had her when he frowned and shook his head, waving slightly to tell her to break off contact with the bodyguard she was plainly walking toward.

The club catered to everyone, from the college-aged vacationers to the senior set. Picking a likely victim from them was harder, but Lauren finally decided on a man and woman in their fifties. The woman obviously didn't care for the way some of the girls were dressed and kept making comments to her husband, who was already three sheets to the wind. She would be the type to squawk the loudest when something went wrong.

The man paid in cash when the drinks came, reaching inside his jacket to pull out his wallet.

Lauren timed her passage by the man as a server came along at the same time. They had to navigate the narrow space between tables.

"Oh. I'm sorry. I wasn't watching where I was going." Lauren stepped back and *accidentally* tripped herself, bumping into the man and falling against him.

Even though he was inebriated, he made a valiant attempt to rescue her. She ended up having to save herself but also managed to end up sitting halfway in his lap.

"My word!" The wife's voice was loud and shrill, the perfect kind of voice to draw attention. "Perhaps you've been drinking too much."

"Actually, it's the heels. I'm not used to wearing them." Lauren gave a wan smile and lifted one heel to show off the tall spike. The heels were taller than she normally wore because she was fairly tall already, but she was comfortable in them. She used them in her occasional magic act. "I'm sorry."

"It's okay." The man held on to Lauren. "I've got you. No worries."

The woman smiled and patted Lauren on the hand. "You poor thing. The shoes are beautiful, but perhaps in the future you should stick with ones you can manage."

"I will." Lauren acted as though she had difficulty getting to her feet, and the man gently nudged her up. She waved her right arm, and the bangles slid and gleamed in the light. While the man was helping her, she slipped her hand inside his jacket and glided the wallet free. She twisted it and hid it beneath her clutch. "Thank you. My name is Clarissa."

"Wonderful name." The woman nodded in approval. "My name is Ruth Beebe. This is my husband, Ralph. We're on holiday from Melbourne."

"I thought I recognized that accent." Lauren focused on Ralph. "Thank you for rescuing me, Ralph."

"No worries, miss. No worries. Quite enjoyable, actually." The man gazed after her and smiled hugely, drawing ire from his wife.

Glancing across the room, Lauren saw that Heath was sitting at his table, but he was now accompanied by two college women who were talking with animation. Irritation flared through Lauren, and she pushed it away because she had a man to frame.

In less than five minutes, she'd picked the pockets of three other men. She walked over to the bodyguard, who was hitting on an elegant woman with coffee-colored skin and a French accent. Lauren stepped in behind the man at the bar and ordered a glass of wine. While she waited, she tucked some of the captured wallets into the bodyguard's jacket without him noticing.

After paying the bartender, she started to walk away with the glass of wine in her right hand.

With her left hand, she opened the first wallet she'd gotten and dropped it on the floor as she bumped into the bodyguard. Ralph Beebe's identification and credit cards were loose in the fold where she'd left them. When the wallet it the floor, the contents scattered.

Lauren instantly knelt down. "So sorry. Let me get that for you."

The bodyguard ignored her at first, then noticed the woman he'd been chatting up wasn't enchanted by his reluctance to help out. He knelt down, too, and began gathering the credit cards. "It's okay. Not my wallet."

Lauren picked up the driver's license that plainly showed Ralph Beebe. She glanced over at Ralph with a look of shock. "Ralph, how did your driver's license get all the way over here?"

Ralph shook his head. "Can't be my wallet."

Lauren held up the driver's license. "This is you." Beside her, the bodyguard had frozen, not sure what he'd gotten involved with.

Ruth slapped her husband on the arm. "Don't be an idiot. Check your wallet."

Ralph shook his head. "It's not mine, I tell

you." He reached into his jacket, then looked surprised. "Hey! My wallet is missing!"

Right on cue, Ruth leveled her arm at the bodyguard, pointing at him in accusation. "That man has my husband's wallet! He stole poor Ralph's wallet! Security! *Security!*"

"Hey, wait a minute." The bodyguard stood and raised his hands. "I didn't do anything. I don't know where that wallet came from."

Ruth and Ralph got up from their seats and came over to examine the wallet. Their voices rose, drawing the attention of everyone nearby. Guys in black T-shirts with Security stamped on them rushed toward the group.

Okay, your work here is done. Quietly and quickly, Lauren eased out of the crowd, barely avoiding the security people as they closed in. She headed for Heath's table, trying unsuccessfully to ignore the young women sitting with him.

The two women glanced at her, too, then shut up and tried to make themselves smaller. One of them looked as if she wanted to say something, but the other woman yanked on her arm and whispered something in her ear. Together, they got up and left, taking their drinks with them.

Heath remained sitting, his attention riveted on the situation rapidly escalating at the front of the club. "What did you do?"

"I'm still trying to find out who killed my sister. Are you interested, or are you taking the evening off?" Lauren knew it was a cheap shot and wasn't necessary, but adrenaline was flooding through her body and she couldn't keep quiet.

Heath remained calm and spoke in a level tone. "What did you do?"

Lauren stood there but didn't look back. "Unless I miss my guess, that bodyguard is about to be arrested for being a pickpocket."

"You framed him with that wallet."

"And with others that are going to be found on him when the police come."

"Why?"

"To separate him from the others. I got him away from them. Do you think you can find out when they let him go?"

Heath was silent for a minute, thinking, watching her with those green-flaked gold eyes. "Yeah. I can do that."

"Then maybe we can find out more about Gibson." Lauren walked toward the exit then, not wanting to be recognized by Ruth and Ralph. She still felt bad about getting them involved in the situation. She just hoped it would be worth it and that Heath could seal the deal on his end.

Chapter 10

"**S**he framed this guy with wallets she'd pick-pocketed from other club guests?" Jackson Port-man sounded incredulous at the other end of the phone connection. "And nobody tripped to that?"

"Yeah." Heath sat behind the wheel of a van he'd "rented" from the same uncle of the kid who had sold him the gun. He'd also paid to have the vehicle detailed and "lost" after he'd finished using it for tonight's soiree.

Jackson laughed uproariously. "Buddy, you have *got* to bring this woman back to 'Lanta. I want to meet her."

Irritation flared through Heath. He didn't want to be around Lauren Cooper any longer than he had to, and he wished she wasn't here now. Mostly. She had a lot of brass, and she was beautiful. "No, you don't want to meet her. She's trouble."

"Trouble? Sounds like she set up a situation where you can have a little personal session with one of Gibson's errand boys."

"She framed him for stealing."

"Says the guy who's patiently waiting outside the city lockup to kidnap the same man. Even in Jamaica they frown on kidnapping a lot more than they do stealing. Or framing someone."

Heath knew he couldn't argue that. He'd gotten the van, duct tape and a black hood for that very purpose. "I can't let the opportunity pass by. But that's only if the guy gets out on his own. If he has one of the other men pick him up, things will get harder."

"You gonna back off if that happens?"

"No."

"Okay, now this ain't so funny." Jackson's voice grew more serious. "One guy, with surprise on your side, I can see how you might think you can get this done. But these guys are military trained, Heath, not the chowderheads we deal with on the street. They ain't nobody to jack around with."

"Yeah, I get that." Heath fingered the lead-filled blackjack lying on the seat beside his thigh.

"You and me have done some cowboy stuff before, buddy, but it was only as we needed to."

"Need to do this now."

"I know you feel that way."

"Not just feel, *know* I have to." Heath stared through the bug-smeared windshield at the exit from the police lockup. It was three in the morning, and the streets were dark in this section of the city. "I'm not getting any closer to Gibson doing this any other way."

"I know, I know. Believe me, I feel you. Where's your girl?"

"She's not my girl." The response came out hotter than Heath expected.

"Touch a nerve there, partner?"

Heath sighed. "She's complicating everything. It is hard enough watching Gibson, trying to figure out what he's doing, without trying to look out for her, too. She doesn't know what she's doing, and now I'm getting stretched thin trying to guess what she might do, too. This thing tonight caught me completely off guard."

"I like what she's doing so far."

"I don't."

"Maybe you need to take the crankypants off and accept the fact that she gave you this guy."

"For all I know, Gibson's going to send a small army down here to get him."

"Crankypants and Debbie Downer. You're falling apart. No matter what, she made something happen tonight. Changed the status quo. You and I both know that's worth something."

"I know."

"You got a guy on the inside of the jail there who's gonna let you know the score on the release?"

"Yeah. FBI agent I talked to when I got down here gave me the name of a jailer that can be bought. Information can be hard to get down here. Sometimes persons of interest pursued by the FBI get *accidentally* released before the agents can pick them up."

"Sounds like the system works both ways."

"It does. I'm just hoping tonight that it works my way. Since the man is from out of country and there's home field advantage, I'm thinking I have a good chance."

"I seen this guy's jacket." Jackson sounded intensely serious now. "Guy's a killer. All of Gibson's so-called security people appear to be."

"They have something in common. Only they kill for money. Gibson kills for something else."

Adrenaline flowing into his body and his pulse rate quickening, Heath spotted his target. "Showtime."

Jackson's chair squeaked at the other end of the connection. "I wish I was there, buddy."

"Me, too."

"Let me know when you're outta the fire."

"Yeah." Heath folded the phone and put it into his pocket. He reached into the passenger seat for the black full facemask and pulled it on. Only his eyes were visible. He fisted the blackjack and opened the door. He'd already extracted the courtesy light from the dome so the vehicle's interior remained dark.

He slipped across the street and hid in the shadows with the blackjack lying along his leg. The exit from the building was just around the corner. A car sped along the darkened street, the pools of light from the headlights momentarily tearing holes in the night.

The man, Vincent Sisco, reached the sidewalk talking on a cell phone. "Yeah, yeah, I'm out. Send somebody to get me." He lifted his head and looked around. "Yeah, well, he ain't *here.* I'm here, but he ain't here, Roylston. I know 'cause I'm standing out here tired and hungry and there ain't nobody else out there." He swore. "I'll call him. He's probably at a joint nearby."

Sisco put his phone away for a moment, then stood long enough to light a cigarette behind cupped hands. He inhaled deeply and blew smoke out as he walked away from Heath. He was cursing as he punched numbers on the cell phone.

Heath followed quickly, hating the fact that the man had gone away from him instead of coming to him. Tension rattled through him as he closed the distance faster than he would have liked to. He stepped carefully, avoiding making any noise, but men out on the battlefield developed a sixth sense about being hunted. Heath's own combat readiness had saved him more than once in Atlanta's alleys.

Vincent Sisco evidently had the same internal warning system. Heath knew that he'd made no noise, that the shadows were falling the other way from the streetlight up ahead, but Sisco turned toward him anyway and dropped into a martial arts crouch.

Heath could hear Jackson's mocking voice in his head as he squared off with his intended prey. *Last thing you needed tonight, brother, a Jackie Chan wannabe.*

Only Sisco wasn't a wannabe. He had the skills, and he wasn't shy about using them. The bodyguard threw a short left jab at Heath's throat, going for the soft spots, not the face. Heath got his right hand up in time to block the blow with his forearm. The impact partially numbed his arm all the way to the elbow.

Sisco followed up with a roundhouse right kick into Heath's side that knocked the wind from his lungs and might have cracked a rib or two. The guy was *fast.* Even as Heath got himself set, the guy unfurled a left snap kick aimed at his groin. Sidestepping to his right, synching into the man's frenetic rhythm, Heath dodged the kick, then avoided the short jab at his throat again, managing to catch Sisco's arm in his left and holding on to it.

Before his opponent could yank his arm free, Heath hammered Sisco's shoulder with the black-jack. The limb went limp in Heath's grip, and he released his hold on it. Face racked with pain, Sisco raised his right leg in another roundhouse kick, this one aimed at Heath's head. Heath blocked with his left arm, feeling the pain digging deep into his side, then brought the black-jack down onto Sisco's thigh.

The man cried out in pain. When he dropped his leg down again and tried to get it to take his weight, the limb crumpled beneath him, and he fell forward. Instinctively, Heath caught the man, roping an arm around the man's chest, then was fighting for his life again as Sisco jabbed fingers at his eyes.

Heath jerked his head, avoiding the cruel fingers, and head-butted the man in the face, feeling Sisco's nose snap. As the man staggered back on his one good leg, Heath swung the blackjack again, catching his opponent under the ear this time.

Sisco's eyes rolled white, and he fell. This

time, Heath let the man fall, not wanting to touch him again until he was certain Sisco was unconscious. As the man lay there, a car came around the street at the end of the block, the lights gleaming against the office buildings. The vehicle cruised slowly while the brake lights lit up intermittently.

On the ground beside Sisco, the dropped cell phone started ringing.

Heath had no doubts that the car slowly coming this way was Sisco's ride. Unwilling to give up his prize so easily, Heath scooped up the phone, dropped it into his pocket, and pulled Sisco up over his shoulder. Before he could start back to the parked van, the car's engine accelerated, and the vehicle braked to a screeching halt out in the street beside Heath.

"Hey!" The driver got out and stood behind the open door. He aimed a large pistol across the top of the car. "Stop right there!"

Heath turned slowly, not certain what his next step was. If the jailers came out of the building, things were going to get even worse.

Another engine roared to life, then Heath watched in disbelief as the van he'd acquired for the night jumped into motion and sped straight at the car. Panicked, the driver whirled and fired two shots at the approaching van, which was gaining speed.

The van plowed into the car, knocking it back several feet. The driver went backward and down, firing one more shot into the air, then he was hanging on to the door as the car skidded back the way it had come.

Heath stared at the bullet holes over the van's driver's side window, totally expecting whoever had been driving to have been shot. Instead, Lauren Cooper's head popped up and looked frantically around as the van rocked to a stop.

Her wide eyes focused on Heath. "Get in!"

My God, you're crazy! Heath couldn't believe she had just done what she'd done, but he started moving on autopilot. The adrenaline spiking his body gave him extra strength and speed, and he jogged over to the van. He popped the side door and shoved his unconscious burden inside, clambering over the man a moment later.

"Are you all right?" Lauren twisted around in her seat and looked at him.

"Me? That guy was shooting at you." Heath flailed out a hand for the roll of duct tape, caught it, then rose on his knees and peered through the windshield.

"I know." Lauren looked at the unconscious man on the floor of the van. "Are you kidnapping that man?"

Heath rolled Sisco over and pulled his hands behind his back, then started taping his wrists together. "No, I'm wrapping him for Christmas."

"You can't just kidnap him!" She stared at him in disbelief.

On the other side of the windshield, the driver started getting to his feet. The interior light streaming from the car revealed his search for the pistol he'd dropped.

"You going to let him start shooting again?" Heath pushed himself to his feet and crouch-walked toward the front two seats.

She shoved the transmission into Reverse and floored the accelerator. The van's engine had demonstrated more power than Heath had expected, and he guessed that this wasn't the first one his contact had supplied for nefarious purposes.

Caught off guard, Heath lost his footing and smashed against the windshield. Before he could recover, Lauren straight-armed him in the side, hitting the same injured ribs the captured man had given him. He cried out in pain just as the driver fired two more shots. One of the rounds punched through the windshield and whistled through the space where he'd just been. The other whistled off the van's nose.

The jail's door opened, and uniformed men peered outside. They had automatic weapons and brandished them with authority.

"Halt!"

Heath dropped into the passenger seat and grabbed for the safety belt. The van started slowing. He pulled the belt around him and stared at Lauren. "What are you doing?"

Both hands on the steering wheel, Lauren looked at the jailers. "They're the police."

"Yeah, they are. And they're going to be really interested in what we're doing out here. Especially after they find out about him." Heath jerked his thumb over his shoulder.

"I didn't kidnap him."

"I don't think they're going to be happy with people driving over pedestrians in the street, either."

"That guy started shooting."

"Go!" Heath placed his foot on top of hers and floored the accelerator again, hoping she kept control of the vehicle.

Startled into action, Lauren looked back over her shoulder and somehow managed to keep the van between the buildings and shot across the intersection. Cars narrowly missed them. Horns blared and brake lights flared ruby all around them.

"Now forward."

Lauren took her foot off the accelerator and placed it on the brake. Once the van had stopped, she put the transmission into Drive and looked at the traffic light in front of them.

Heath gazed around, wondering what she was seeing. "What are you waiting for?"

"The light's red."

Despite the fear that was thundering through him, Heath couldn't help laughing. Sometimes that happened when things got tense. During those times, Jackson Portman swore that Heath was insane.

The laughter evidently touched a nerve. Lauren shoved her foot down on the accelerator and swerved to the right, narrowly avoiding locking bumpers with a car in the oncoming lane. She also cursed at him. "There's nothing funny about this."

Heath shifted in the seat, trying to find a comfortable position because the ribs were aching something fierce at the moment, but that pursuit was made even more impossible by the safety belt and Lauren's erratic driving.

"I know, I know. Sorry. But it was kind of funny at the time."

Lauren got the van straightened out, and they hurtled down the street for two blocks. Then she forced her breath out and spoke without looking at him. "The police are going to be after us. I don't want to be arrested. And I don't know where I'm going." Her voice sounded ragged and hard.

"It's okay. I do." Heath knew she was on the verge of losing it. Truthfully, he didn't know how she'd done everything she'd already done.

He'd had a lot of experience in the military as a soldier and in Atlanta as a police officer and detective. His younger years hadn't been spent without incident, either. "I know where we're going."

"Okay." Lauren took a breath and relaxed a little.

"We're going to be fine. At the next intersection, take another right."

"Okay."

"And you can slow down a little."

Lauren nodded and eased off the accelerator. She made the turn, and Heath kept watch for any signs of pursuit.

Chapter 11

"I can't believe you *kidnapped* that man." Lauren stood with her arms crossed in an alley in a part of Kingston that she knew she wouldn't have visited during the daylight. She was certain rats patrolled the overflowing garbage bin, and from the raw stink that filled the air between the warehouses near the harbor, she felt positive that bodies had been left there.

She didn't want to be there. More than anything, though, she wished she could stop shaking. Now that everything seemed to be over, now that there was no more shooting and it looked as though they had escaped police pursuit, she felt as if she was going to be sick. She didn't want to think about how close the bullets had come.

Bullets. She couldn't believe she'd even thought that.

"Me?" Heath slid the van's side door open with a rasping squeak that sounded loud enough to broadcast for miles. He was irritatingly cool and collected by comparison. "You framed this guy and got him arrested. You wanted me to talk to him, right?"

"Yes. *Talk* to him. Not kidnap him." Lauren hadn't envisioned that Heath would act so directly.

"Seriously? How was I supposed to get him to talk to me?" Heath sounded as if he was torn between anger and incredulity. "This guy is a trained mercenary and works for a man we think is a serial killer, and he gets busted for something he *knows* he didn't do, and somehow that's going to persuade him to become my best friend so he'd reveal all his boss's dirty secrets?"

Lauren hesitated, knowing, even though the kidnapping was beyond what she had imagined Heath would do, what she had imagined had been close. "I thought maybe you'd rough him up a little."

"'Rough him up?' How, exactly, is that different from kidnapping him?"

Lauren glared at him, for the moment hating the logic he was insisting on. "It's not *kidnapping*. It's…different."

Heath snorted and leaned in to check his prisoner. The man was still unconscious.

Worried, Lauren leaned in. "Are you sure he's breathing?"

"Yes, I'm sure he's breathing."

"You hit him pretty hard."

"I didn't hit him any harder than I needed to. I know what I'm doing."

"You routinely kidnap people?"

"No, I don't routinely kidnap people. But I've subdued perps before, and I've knocked out a few guys."

Lauren didn't know how to react to that.

Heath pulled back out of the van and momentarily his body was pushed up against hers because she hadn't noticed him shifting until he was there.

Pressed against him, Lauren felt the tension in

him, felt the hard planes of his back and the taut muscles of his shoulders. She'd gotten the impression of strength when she'd struggled with him at the morgue, but he felt different now. There was something more feral about him. At this moment, he fit in this alley and in this dark part of the world.

Shocked a little, Lauren drew back and stumbled. Heath caught her by the shoulder, hand moving so fast that she didn't even see it in motion. His steely fingers stopped just short of biting into the flesh of her upper arm.

"Are you okay?" The anger was gone from his voice now, only concern sounded in there, and those green-flecked gold eyes softened.

"Yes. I'm fine." She wanted to shove his hand away, but he guided her a couple steps back to the driver's seat.

"Why don't you sit down? I suspect tonight has been a bit much."

"It's my first kidnapping." Reluctantly, Lauren sat. Once he was sure she was settled, Heath pulled back and looked at her.

"You didn't get hurt when you crashed into that car, did you?"

She shook her head. "I don't think so. I don't feel hurt. I just got light-headed there for a second."

"Adrenaline overload. You'll be all right in a few minutes." Heath reached into the back of the van and handed her a bottle of water. "Here. Drink this."

Almost childlike, Lauren uncapped the bottle and drank. Her lips quivered, and some of the water dribbled down her chin.

Heath stood in front of her, watching over her and the—*their*—prisoner. "How did you get there tonight?"

She stared at him. "Do you really think we have time to go into this now?"

With a nonchalant air, Heath leaned against the van. "We have to wait for Sleeping Beauty to wake up."

"You're just going to question him here? In the alley?"

"Yes. I don't want him to know for certain who has him. Which is why I was wearing this." Heath plucked the black mask from his back pocket. He frowned as he regarded her. "I don't want him to recognize you, either." He reached back into the van, pulled a strip of duct tape from the roll on the floor, and strapped it across the man's eyes. "When he wakes up, I'm going to ask the questions. You keep quiet. Gibson and his security people might guess that I had a hand in this, but they don't need to know about you. Now, how did you get there tonight?"

Lauren shot him a look. "The police arrested him. He was going to jail. I figured you would be here, so I came along."

"To do what?"

"To see if you…talked to him."

"What were you going to do while I *talked* to him?"

"Wait. Then talk to you and find out what you'd discovered."

Heath held up a Baggie that contained a cell phone, wallet, coins and paper money and keys. "Not much. Guy travels light."

Lauren studied the bag. "That's a smartphone. He's probably got numbers and maybe even an itinerary on it."

"That's why I took it."

"Then they'll know that you know." Lauren shook her head. "You should copy whatever information you find there, then put the phone back so he won't know you've looked at it. That way—" She stopped when she realized Heath was just looking at her. "What?"

"Are you sure this is your first kidnapping?" He was smiling at her.

She grimaced impatiently. "The kind of trouble we're in, and you think this is funny?"

"It kind of is, yeah. You're the one with the big idea of talking to this guy, now you just want to give him back. For all you know, this guy helps Gibson kill his victims."

That hurt. For a moment Lauren had a brief vision of Megan struggling against her captors in the water. Heath was right. Even if the man hadn't helped Gibson, there was little doubt that the man knew what kind of monster he had for an employer.

"Sorry." Heath shook his head. "My partner thinks I've got a twisted sense of humor. At the wrong times. Janet used to say the same thing." He took the smartphone from the Baggie and started it up.

The view screen lit up, standing out brightly in the dark alley. Several small eyes in the garbage reflected the illumination. Lauren tried not to think about that.

"The phone's pass-code protected." Heath growled and started to drop the phone back into the Baggie. "I'll have to keep it and see if I can get someone to scrape the information off the SIM card."

"Do you think you're going to find anything on that card?"

"Don't know till I try."

"I can't see this man leaving pictures of previous murders on his phone." A chill chased through Lauren. "Or even taking pictures of something like that."

"Men like Gibson, men like these mercenaries, they're not wired like your average person, Lauren. That's something you need to know about them." Heath frowned at her. "Especially if you're going to continue to play in their sandbox."

"I'm not playing in their sandbox. I'm trying to find out who killed my sister."

"I know." Heath regarded her levelly. "Something else you should know—I'll do *anything* it takes to find the man who killed Janet and those other women. And I won't let anyone stand in the way."

The wind slipping through the alley seemed to drop a few degrees as she looked at him. She knew that he meant it. If she hadn't been convinced that Gibson had killed Megan, she would have been worried that Heath might let his pain and loss blind him to the point that he would persecute an innocent man. But she was convinced of Gibson's guilt, as well.

The unconscious man inside the van rolled slightly, moaned and turned his head.

Heath put a finger to his lips, then turned his full attention to the prisoner. He knotted a fist in the man's shirt and jerked him up to a sitting position in the open van door.

"Sisco, do you hear me?" Heath's voice was calm and flat, barely loud enough to carry.

"Is that you, cop? You got that redneck accent I can hear. You better kill me, 'cause when I get loose, I'm gonna kill you." Sisco leaned forward and spat at Heath.

Heath easily dodged, then yanked the man hard to one side, banging his head against the door frame.

The man cursed and started squirming in pain, and Lauren felt even more scared when she realized the man knew who Heath was.

Heath waited till the man's cries subsided. His voice remained level when he spoke. "Nobody said you were getting out of this alive, Sisco. If you don't answer my questions, I'm going to put a bullet in your head and drop you out in the ocean. The crabs and the gulls can finish off what's left of you."

Lauren knew that Heath wouldn't do that; at least, she trusted him not to do that, but the threat made everything worse.

"Roylston will know you grabbed me, and he'll figure I told you everything I know. He'll kill me if you don't."

Lauren thought she was going to be sick. She hadn't thought about that possibility at all.

"Then you've got nothing to lose by telling me what you know."

Sisco shook his head. "Man, you grabbed the wrong guy. You wanted the whole story, you shoulda grabbed Roylston. All I know is that Gibson likes killing women."

"And you just let him? Is that what you're saying? You just let him kill those women?" The words were out of Lauren's mouth before she knew she was going to speak.

Sisco sniffed. "I know that perfume. You're the woman who's so free with everybody else's wallets." He shook his head and winced. "I gotta say, that was pretty slick the way you set me up. Never saw it coming. Did you put her up to that, cop?"

"Tell me about Gibson."

"What's to tell?"

"Why does he kill the women?"

Sisco shrugged. "Guy's sick. Twisted. If you've been in the military, you've seen guys like him. Probably seen them in Atlanta, too."

Lauren couldn't help herself. "Why are you working for him?"

"Money's good, and Gibson doesn't kill as many people as other employers I've had. You ask me, this is one of the easier assignments I've had. Roylston makes this operation run like goose grease on ice. Keeps us all tight and right."

At the end of the alley, a car rushed by, then brakes squealed and white reverse lights flared to life. An engine roared as the car pulled back to the alley, then changed directions and raced down it.

Smiling, Sisco looked in Heath's direction. "That'll be Roylston. He keeps tabs on everybody. Hope he doesn't kill you too quick."

Instinctively, Lauren ducked down, and it was just ahead of a fusillade of bullets that struck the rear of the van. Broken glass tumbled from the windows. A man hung out the window of the approaching car and fired repeatedly.

It took her a moment, but she thought she recognized the bodyguard who had been sitting with Gibson at the restaurant a couple of days ago. The muzzle flashes highlighted his face for a moment before she ducked below the door and lost sight of him.

The bullets ricocheted off the van and the building walls. At least one of them crashed through Sisco's head in a spray of blood, and he fell back inside the van.

Warm wetness splashed against the side of Lauren's face. She reached up and wiped at it. Her fingers came away stained with crimson, and she almost screamed.

Heath pulled Lauren's upper arm, getting her

into motion and keeping her low. He pushed her to keep her moving. "Keep going. Get to the end of the alley. I'll be right behind you."

Frightened, Lauren did as she was told because she couldn't think of anything else to do. Bullets whined off the wall overhead and crashed through the trash cans.

Then heavier *cracks* punctuated the automatic fire. Lauren glanced back over her shoulder and saw Heath firing from behind the open driver's door. In the next instant, he turned and charged toward her, easily overtaking her and grabbing her by the arm again.

"C'mon!"

Lauren ran, somehow matching him stride for stride till they reached the end of the alley. Heath paused at the corner with his back against the wall. Without looking, he opened the revolver and shook the hot brass into his hand, dropping it into his jacket pocket and bringing out new shells, inserting them into the cylinder, then snapping the cylinder closed again.

Peering around his shoulder, Lauren saw the other vehicle had stopped in front of the van, unable to proceed any farther. At least two men climbed out of the car because their weapons flickered lightning on both sides of the alley. Neither of them appeared to be in any hurry to pursue Heath and Lauren.

Heath whirled around and looked at the street as a taxi came up it. He grabbed Lauren's hand and pulled her out into the street, waving to cut the taxi off. She assumed the driver didn't see the gun in Heath's hand, because the vehicle came to a stop beside them.

Opening the door, Heath pushed her inside. Instinct took over, and she climbed in willingly. Heath dropped into the seat beside her and addressed the driver, giving him the name of a club downtown.

Lauren turned to him as the taxi pulled away from the curb and the two shadows halted at the alley mouth. "Where are we going? We need to go to the police!" That caught the taxi driver's attention, and he glanced up at the rearview mirror. "We can't just—"

Heath leaned in and kissed her, taking her breath away and shorting out her senses. She wanted to push him off her, might have even tried, but he twisted in the seat and wrapped his arms around her, holding her tight. The immediate panic passed, and she gave herself over to the kiss, losing herself in it. A fire ignited in her belly, and she knew it had been there for the past couple days. Fear swirled into hunger, and she lifted her hand and cupped the back of his head, pulling him in close because having him there made her feel alive, and she knew she'd come close to not being alive.

He opened his mouth, demanded access to her, and she gave it willingly, surprised at the appetite that threatened to consume her in a rush. He tasted sweet and strong and masculine, and he growled as his own need flowered within him, too.

His hand drifted down her body, pulling her closer, drifting farther down till he cupped her hip and held on tight. She put her other hand on his jaw, feeling the rough, sandpapery stubble that covered his chin. For the moment, all that mattered was having him close, but that was triggering a greater need in her she didn't want to address.

Out of air, needing to breathe, Lauren pulled back from Heath. After a quick breath, he came after her again, but she noticed that the taxi driver was paying more attention to the rear-view mirror than to the street. The shadows must have hidden the blood on her face.

"No." Lauren slid a hand over his mouth and blocked his attempts to kiss her again. "No."

Reluctantly, Heath pulled back against the seat as if it took all his strength to do that. "Okay." Lights from passing streetlamps and businesses that were still open flashed in his gold eyes and caught on the green flakes. "Maybe we can talk about the other thing later."

Not trusting herself to speak, Lauren nodded.

Once they arrived at the club Heath had suggested, he paid the driver and took Lauren's hand. They walked three blocks through the downtown party area and stayed in the shadows. Heath kept checking behind them, but he didn't act as if anyone was following them.

At the corner, he flagged down another taxi and told the driver to take them back to the jail.

Chapter 12

Surprisingly, there was no real activity at the jail building. Lauren had expected a gathering of police cars, emergency vehicles and fire trucks as there were in movies and television shows. Instead, only a spray of broken glass marked the area where she'd driven the van into the car.

Heath caught her looking around and squeezed her hand. "The police won't be here. They'll be working the murder in the alley."

"The murder." Lauren repeated the words and still had trouble wrapping her mind around it.

"Yeah. Those guys murdered Sisco. They were there to take out everyone."

"That doesn't make any sense."

"They were trying to kill us. Sisco was just collateral damage. We got lucky."

It wasn't just luck. Heath had gotten them moving quickly, too.

"What are you driving?"

Mechanically, functioning on fumes of adrenaline now, Lauren pointed out the compact rental she'd arranged.

Still holding on to her arm as if they were out for a night on the town, Heath walked them over to the vehicle. "Let me have your keys."

Lauren thought briefly of arguing with him, of telling him she was capable of driving, then she decided it wasn't worth the effort. She handed the keys over. Heath opened the passenger door and put her inside, then slid behind the wheel, and they were off.

At the hotel where Lauren was staying, Heath pulled the car into the outside parking lot, then got out with her and led the way toward the building. The hotel was set back from the main streets, and darkness surrounded them. On previous nights, the darkness hadn't bothered Lauren, but now it felt almost threatening as she crossed the short expanse of pavement to the side entrance.

She was walking better, more focused. "I can make it to my room."

"I can walk you." Heath was distracted, looking all around them.

No one was in the mezzanine when they entered the hotel. Lauren's stomach clenched as they crossed the open area, expecting to be apprehended at any moment. She felt almost relieved when they stepped into the elevator.

Heath's hand hesitated over the buttons. "What floor?"

"Five." Lauren glanced at her reflection in the stainless-steel panels that covered the doors. She had something on her face. Her skin felt tight. Automatically, she reached up to brush at her cheek.

Heath caught her hand and trapped it gently. "Don't."

She looked at him, swallowed hard, and tried not to freak out when she realized what the dark splotches were. "I've got his blood on my face."

"Not for long."

That wasn't any kind of answer. Lauren wanted

it *off.* Now. She clenched her fist and willed her-self not to touch her face, but she couldn't help glancing down and seeing more blood spattered over the black pullover she was wearing.

"Just stay calm. We're almost there."

She made herself nod, but her breathing was strained.

"Where's your room key?"

Grateful for something else to think about, something else to do, Lauren slipped the key card to her room from the back pocket of her jeans. She handed it to Heath and let him guide her to one side of the door.

"I need you to stay back just a minute." He had his pistol in hand, covered by the loose folds of his jacket, when he slipped the key card through the slot. When the light flashed green, he pulled the lever down with his left hand and leaned a shoulder into the door. He relaxed a little and turned to her. "Okay." He stepped to the side so she could enter. "Does anything look moved? Touched in any way?"

Lauren entered the room and looked around. Her suitcases were in the closet, her iPad on the desk on the charger, and her clothing was hung as she'd left it. "No. Everything's fine."

"Good. I don't think they know about you, but I didn't think they'd have a tracker on Sisco, either. I don't want to be surprised again tonight." Heath slid the pistol back into the holster on his hip.

Pausing in front of the mirror at the vanity, Lauren looked at herself, shocked at the blood that marred the side of her face, her neck and her hair. She didn't know how the taxi drivers had missed seeing that. Then she thought maybe the man hadn't and that the Kingston constables were already en route.

She grabbed a handful of tissues from the box in the vanity and started scrubbing at the blood on her cheek, but it wouldn't come off because it was dried. She started to shake then, and she scrubbed even harder.

"Hey." Heath stood behind her. "Calm down."

"Calm down?" She glared at him in the mirror, unable to stop scrubbing. "I've got someone's blood on me. It's in my *hair*."

"It'll wash out." Gently, Heath took her hands

and kept her from scrubbing. "Take a shower. Everything's going to be all right."

She looked at him, wishing she could believe him, but he had blood on his face, too. Both of them had been *so* close to dying. She closed her eyes and saw the man getting shot again, his head snapping back, feeling the warm wetness on her face.

"Get some clothes. Take a shower. You'll feel better."

Lauren just looked at him, not believing that he thought a shower was going to fix everything. When she didn't move, he went to the chest of drawers and began searching through them.

Watching him paw through her underwear broke her out of her trance. "What are you doing?"

"You need clothing."

"Stay out of there."

Heath ignored her, emerging with a pair of panties, sweat pants and an oversized T-shirt, all things that she liked to lounge in and sleep in. He handed them to her. "Here."

Not knowing what else to do, Lauren took the proffered clothing.

"Shower." Heath gave her a gentle shove to get her moving.

"Aren't you leaving?"

Heath looked at her and spoke softly. "No. I'm not leaving. I'm going to be right here."

For a moment, Lauren remembered the kisses in the taxi. Her body still thrummed with excitement, but it was mixed in with the residual aftereffects of the near-miss in the alley. She felt confused, not certain what Heath's motives were.

He turned from her, though, and walked to the window. He stripped his jacket off and dropped it onto the chair by the small table, then moved a chair so he could more easily peer out the window as well as watch the news on the television he angled his way.

Not knowing what else to do, lost amid all the conflicting emotions, Lauren retreated to the bathroom. She took off her clothing with shaking hands, feeling terribly cold all of a sudden. Then she stepped under the shower spray and turned it up as hot as she could bear. For a long time, she just stood there and let the wet heat seep into her. She turned her face up to the spray and let it run through her hair, not looking down to see if the blood was sluicing from her body.

With her eyes shut against the shower, she kept seeing the gunfire again and again, but mixed in there, she kept feeling Heath's lips pressed against hers.

"Heath?" Jackson Portman sounded tense. "Buddy, I was about to give up on you getting back to me."

"Told you I'd call." Heath sat in the chair looking through the window out at the parking lot. Nothing was moving. The street out in front of the hotel only had occasional traffic.

"Get anything?"

"Gibson is our guy. The man we took down tonight—Sisco—confirmed that Gibson is killing the women."

"Wait a minute. *We?*"

"Yeah. Lauren worked herself into the snatch. Saved my butt, actually, but everything went sideways on us." As Heath relayed the story, he couldn't help thinking about Lauren in the shower. The water ran steadily, and he knew it was tracing every curve. He kept thinking about the kisses in the taxi, as well. He'd kissed her to shut her down, to keep her from speaking. At least, that was what it had started out being. At the end there, he wasn't sure what that was about, but she had seemed to be getting into it.

"This guy Roylston was the one that pulled the trigger?"

Heath played the scene over in his mind again. There had been too many variables in play. He hadn't been expecting to be found, hadn't been expecting Lauren to be there, and he hadn't expected everything to turn so violent so quickly. His first instinct had been to get Lauren safe, not identify the shooters.

But he felt certain he'd seen Roylston's face revealed in the muzzle flashes.

"Yeah, I think so. Things happened pretty fast once they arrived."

"Sisco getting dropped like that is gonna send a message to the rest of Gibson's bodyguards. They're all expendable."

"I know, but something about the shooting doesn't feel right."

"What do you mean?"

"Back at the jail, Sisco's partner came to pick

him up. If he'd been worried about Sisco talking, he could have opened fire on both of us."

"Maybe Lauren ran the van into him before he could."

"No. He had time to shoot. He was trying to protect his partner. Doesn't make sense that he would kill him so easily a few minutes later."

"His partner probably got picked up by the police out in front of the jail. He probably wasn't even there, so he didn't have a say."

"Maybe not, but his response felt different than those guys back in the alley. Roylston and his crew came to kill somebody."

"Could be you triggered that reaction out of Gibson by confronting him."

"This wasn't Gibson. He's too interested in gaming me. He's a guy who wants to taunt every chance he gets, then slide the knife in slow. If you met him, I bet you'd read him the same way. This thing tonight was a burn. Roylston, if that was him, was happy to sacrifice one of the bodyguards in an attempt to get me."

"That doesn't make sense."

"It does if Roylston doesn't like the way Gibson is dealing with me. The guy's got the money and the connections, Jackson. He could be in the wind, gone too far and too fast for me to follow. My pockets aren't as deep as his. He could leave me at the starting gate. Instead, it's like he's baiting me."

"All the more reason to regroup and bring it home, buddy."

"I know. I'm giving that some serious thought." Heath gazed back at the bathroom. "I need to get Lauren clear of this whole mess before she gets hurt."

"Good. Because I'd like you to come home, too."

Heath peered out into the darkness, but he wasn't seeing it. He was seeing that crime scene with Janet. "This guy killed Janet. I can't let him get away with it."

"He's not going to get away with it, bro. You know you've got the right guy. Now it's just a matter of police work."

"Police work's not going to reach from Atlanta."

"We'll find something. We'll keep turning things over till we do."

"You and I both know that the captain put everything we could into that investigation. There was nothing at that scene that ties to Gibson. We don't even know what his real name is, and without probable cause, we won't be able to get it. We haven't been able to get through his lawyers."

"I know, but I also know all of this takes time."

"I'm putting pressure on him here. Things are happening."

Jackson sighed. "You're gonna get hurt there, Heath. That woman is going to get hurt. You don't want that to happen."

Heath didn't reply, but he knew it was true. Protecting Lauren Cooper was becoming very important to him.

"You put enough pressure on Gibson down there that you almost got killed. This guy isn't going to let anyone interfere with his games, and he's got a group of heavy hitters working for him. You've seen their rap sheets same as I have. They're not guys you want to meet in dark alleys."

"They won't get me again like that. The tracker surprised me."

"Heath, the next time Roylston surprises you, it might be from behind with a bullet into your ear. Step back from the ledge. Get some perspective."

Everything Jackson said made sense. Reluctant as he was, Heath knew it was the right thing to do. "Okay."

The water in the bathroom stopped running.

Heath sat up a little straighter. "I've got to go."

"Fine. Give me a call in the morning. Let me know when I can expect you here."

"Will do." Heath hung up the phone and sat in the darkness crowding the room.

"I'm not leaving." Feeling somewhat refreshed from the shower, Lauren stood in front of Heath. She hadn't known what to expect when she stepped out into the room, but she had certainly not expected him to still be there, though she hadn't liked the idea of him leaving. She just thought he would have.

Heath sat in the chair at the table. His elbows rested on his knees as he leaned toward her. "This isn't about just you leaving this time, Lauren. It's about *us* leaving. It's not safe here. Gibson or Roylston or someone else will be gunning for us."

"You mean, they'll be gunning for you. They don't know I was involved."

"You don't know that."

"They're not here." Lauren hung on to the outrage she felt. That emotion was the only thing getting her through the residual fear left inside her. "If they knew about me, I think they'd be here right now."

"Maybe. And maybe they're biding their time because the heat is on them right now because of Sisco."

She shook her head. "You're not going to scare me. I'm not going to let you."

"Now is the time to be scared." Heath spoke in a level tone that Lauren hated. He was making too much sense. "This response tonight, it was way more than anything I figured would happen. Gibson is hitting hard and fast."

"That's fine. That's what we want him to do, right?" Lauren knew she was right and held to her conviction. "Come at us and make a mistake?" She thought hurriedly. "In fact, can't that shooting in the alley be used against him? Aren't the police going to investigate him because one of his people was killed?" A chill ghosted through her as she said that. She wrapped her arms around herself to stay warm. The heat from the shower was already leaving her, but she was still hypersensitive to Heath's presence.

He pointed at the television. "Gibson's people have already got their story in place. Sisco was grabbed outside the jail by persons unknown. Gibson's lawyers say he doesn't know anything about it and random acts of violence aren't his responsibility. Since Gibson has nothing to do with the case, he's not going to get involved."

"What?" Lauren couldn't believe it.

"The police can't do anything but question Gibson about his employee. There's nothing to tie Sisco's death to him."

"Gibson's people killed that man."

"Maybe."

"I saw Gibson's bodyguard there. He was the one firing the gun. I can testify to that."

"Are you sure it was him?"

"Yes. You saw him, too."

"I saw a guy that looked like him. Without physical evidence that concretely says Roylston was there, it would be our word against his. A good attorney will bring up the fact that the alley was dark, that bullets were flying, that the head-lights were in our eyes. Those are all things you can sell a jury on, if it ever got past a judge, and you can bet Gibson's attorneys won't let it go that far."

"If we go in, we can tell them he was the one that killed Sisco. If Roylston knows we've iden-tified him, he might get scared. He could plead out and tell the police Gibson sent him there to kill Sisco in exchange for a reduced sentence."

"Did Gibson send Roylston there? That's a jump. This could be something Roylston did on his own to protect his security perimeter. Or maybe Gibson sells Roylston out and says Roylston was working on his own. Again, this might not roll back over onto Gibson. On top of that, Roylston's a mercenary. He's not going to be able to work in his field if he gives up his employer. He gets paid to take the hits. I think he's going to like his chances of running free better than a trial."

Frustrated, Lauren realized that was true.

"Even if the police believed us and arrested Roylston, he'd be out on bail and gone before his trial. Either he'd be out of the country, or maybe

Gibson would hire someone else to take him out, if he didn't trust him to keep his mouth shut." Heath's voice remained a soft growl. "Even worse than that, if we offer testimony about what Sisco said and the fact that Roylston *might* have been there, we'd have to explain what we were doing there in that alley."

Lauren closed her eyes in defeat. She hadn't thought of that.

"We'd have to admit we kidnapped Sisco. The police know the man was taken. We'd end up in jail before Gibson did. And I don't think any-one would be interested in testimony from ad-mitted kidnappers working on an agenda to pin your sister's murder and my partner's death on Gibson."

"So we're screwed, is that it? We know Gibson did it and we can't touch him." Anger crept up inside Lauren and outweighed the residual fear that caromed inside her.

"Sisco said that Gibson killed those women. But for all we know, he was lying. Maybe he was the killer and was framing Gibson, and Roylston just executed him tonight to put an end to everything. There might not be any more White Rabbit killings."

Lauren pinned him with her gaze. "Do you think the killing is going to stop?"

Heath returned her gaze full measure for a moment, then he blew out a disgusted breath and shook his head. "No. Whoever killed Janet and your sister and all those other women, he's gotten a taste for blood. Could be he's always had it. Whatever the case, it's not going away. I don't believe Sisco was the killer."

"So we're just supposed to pack up and leave? That's your answer?"

Heath spoke softly, rationally, and that came close to infuriating Lauren. "Leaving is the best thing to do." He paused and shook his head. "Believe me, I don't like it any more than you do."

"What happens to the next girl that Gibson goes after?"

"We need to regroup, find a new way to go at this."

"You're just giving him time to kill again. You've already said that his timetable is accelerating. How many women can he kill while we're regrouping?" Lauren answered before

Heath could. "I don't know if you can answer that, but I can tell you this—even one person is too many. You can leave if you want to, but I'm staying."

Slowly, Heath stood and came over to her. "You're a stubborn woman."

"No." Lauren looked up into his eyes, and she remembered the kisses in the back of the taxi. For a minute she thought he was going to try something like that again. "I'm just right, and you know it."

"You are right. So we'll play this out until we've got the answers we're looking for or we're in jail." Heath looked at his watch. "You should get some sleep. Tomorrow's going to start early."

He walked over to the bed, and Lauren briefly thought he intended to stretch out on it, which didn't sound as awkward as it should have. Instead, he pulled a pillow from the bed and crossed the room to the couch. He lay down, kicked off his shoes, and placed the big revolver under his pillow.

"What are you doing?"

"I'm not leaving you alone tonight. That's not happening."

Lauren wanted to protest because she didn't like the idea of Heath invading her space, but she also didn't want to be alone. Reluctantly, she walked to the bed and stripped off the top blanket, then gave it to Heath, surprising him. He didn't say anything, though, and Lauren was glad. She didn't know what he would say, and she definitely didn't know what kind of reply she would make to anything he said.

She returned to the bed, pulled the blanket and sheet back and crawled in before shutting off the lamp. Darkness enveloped them and quietness filled the room.

For a long time, she lay there listening to Heath breathe. After a few minutes, his breathing deepened, and she knew that he had gone to sleep. She felt tired and she wanted to go to sleep, but memory of the shooting and the way Heath had kissed her in the back of the taxi danced in her head, keeping her alert and thinking until sleep finally claimed her.

Chapter 13

Bright sunlight slanting through the heavy curtains woke Lauren. She shifted in bed and tried to doze off again, but then she spotted Heath Sawyer's lanky body overrunning the small couch at both ends and knew she wasn't getting back to sleep anytime soon.

He slept like a kid, on his back with one arm folded over his eyes. Sometime after he'd gone to bed, he'd taken off his shirt and lay there naked to the waist. His body was hard, his chest was broad, chiseled from working out, and the sight of that smooth, bronze skin awakened a hunger in Lauren that she'd never felt before. She made herself look at his face, but she couldn't maintain her concentration.

Giving up, she got out of bed as quietly as she could, knowing that he needed his sleep. He'd been putting in a lot of hours watching over Gibson, and that had gone on for days before she had joined him.

He turned slightly on the couch, and the blanket drifted farther south. That movement caught Lauren's attention, but his shirt hung by itself on the back of a nearby chair, so she guessed that he was still partially dressed. However, the scar on his left side was revealed. It was pale white with age, but stood out against the tan skin and was at least five inches long. She knew it wasn't from an appendectomy, because it was on the wrong side and ran too vertical.

The scar and the tan both made her curious because she wanted to know where he'd gotten them. The tan looked real, gotten from working outside, not from a tanning bed, and a homicide detective didn't often have cause to take his shirt off at work.

Blood spatters had ruined his shirt. Lauren felt a queasy roll in her stomach just for a moment, then she forced the feeling away. She was surprised that no one had noticed the blood last night, but it had been dark. There was no way Heath was going to be able to walk around in daylight without someone calling the police.

And staying in the hotel room all day, as intriguing as that seemed given the sparks that had flared between them last night, wasn't something Lauren was prepared to risk. The hunt for Megan's killer was complicated enough without pursuing whatever that had been, and she was more than willing to admit it was a mistake brought on by adrenaline.

She knew she needed to get out of the room, away from Heath Sawyer, and clear her head. A brief shopping spree would serve as a good distraction.

Lauren grabbed khaki pants and an orange pullover that she knew fit her nicely and flattered her figure. She headed to the bathroom.

Heath's cell phone woke him with a start. He rolled over on the couch, feeling the aches from sleeping in the cramped space, and grabbed the cell from the floor by the couch. He pulled it to his ear. "Hello."

"Good morning, Detective Sawyer. Sleep well?"

At first, Heath didn't recognize the caller because he'd never before heard him on the phone. "Who is this? How did you get this number?"

"It wasn't hard. I got your friend Janet's number, too."

"Gibson." Heath recognized the carefully enunciated words and laid-back tone then. Gibson was giving a performance.

Heath threw the blanket off and sat up on the couch. He pulled his gun from under the pillow and looked at the hotel door. The interior locks were no longer in place. A trickle of fear snaked down his spine. He glanced over at the bed and saw that it had been made.

Lauren was gone.

Heath got to his feet and shouldered the phone. He walked toward the bathroom, fearing what he might find in there. Even though it didn't make sense that Gibson or his men could have gotten into the hotel, much less known where it was, it also didn't make sense that they would kill Lauren and leave him alive.

Except now he's playing games with you. He's moved into a new phase of his killing.

"You can call me whatever name you want to. I'll answer to it."

Heath rounded the corner to the bathroom with his revolver at the ready. He peered into the room, but it was too dark to see the shower. Flipping on the light switch beside him, his pulse beating at his temples, he looked at the shadows created by the white shower curtain.

There was no blood on the floor. If Lauren had been killed like Janet, there would have been blood everywhere. Heath crossed the room and whipped the shower curtain back. When he saw that it was empty, contained none of the horrors he'd imagined, he let out a long breath.

"What do you want, Gibson?" Turning from the shower, Heath padded barefoot back into the room, looking for some indication of what had happened to Lauren.

Since the bed was made, he felt she'd left of her own volition. The neatly made bed also made him realize how soundly he'd slept. He'd stayed the night to protect her. Some bodyguard.

"I regret having missed you last night."

"You didn't miss me. Your people missed me. They didn't miss your buddy Sisco. I didn't see you there last night, so I suppose you keep your killing to women." Heath gripped his pistol tightly and looked around the room, finally turning and spotting a note on the mirror of the vanity outside the bathroom.

Went shopping. Back soon. L.

Shopping? Heath held back a curse and kept himself calm with effort. Last night should have taught Lauren the danger they were in.

"You made a mistake last night." Gibson's anger was apparent in his tone.

"No, I didn't. It's just going to be a matter of time till I bring you down."

"That's what your partner thought, didn't she? It didn't work out for her. It won't work out for you."

Gibson broke the connection before Heath could reply. He checked the view screen and only saw Unavailable there. He tried to reconnect the call, but it kept failing out. Cursing, wishing he knew where Lauren Cooper was, he called Jackson Portman.

"Yeah?" Jackson sound tired.

"Catch you at a bad time?"

"Tell me you're on a plane for 'Lanta and I'll get to feeling better quick."

"Gibson just called me."

"Why?"

"To gloat. Do me a favor—dump the phone records on this number and see if you can trace the phone number that called me this morning. It'll be the only incoming call today. You probably won't get anything, but it's worth trying."

"I can do that. When are you headed home?"

"Not now."

"Seriously?"

"Lauren says she's not leaving. I can't make her go." Heath took a breath. "And it's not just her. I can't leave this thing unfinished, either. We've poked Gibson enough that we've got a reaction."

"'We?' That woman's not a partner, buddy. She's not even a cop. She's a civilian. You're letting her get in harm's way. That's not like you."

"If I leave, she's going to stay. I can't let her stay without protection."

"That's not your problem."

"Would you leave?"

Jackson swore.

"Yeah, I didn't think so. I'm going to protect her, and I'm going to get the answers Janet's family needs."

Jackson was quiet for a moment. "Listen, Heath, you and I both have been around the block a time or two. We know there isn't an answer for what happened to Janet. Gibson's a predator, pure and simple. He kills because he wants to."

"Then I'm going to find a way to put him down. I've got to try to give them that. I owe it to them." Heath stared out the window at the tourists walking the street in front of the hotel. There were enough of them that he guessed one or more of the cruise ships were in the harbor.

"Okay. I'll dump this number, see if we find anything."

"Thanks."

"Where's Lauren Cooper now?"

"I don't know."

"Well…that's not good."

"I know." Heath picked up his shirt from the back of the chair and noticed the dark blood-stains all over it. There was no way he could walk around in that shirt without getting the police called. "Get back to me when you can."

"I will."

Heath punched the phone off and slid it into his pocket. He took the shirt to the vanity sink and poured soap all over it, then started washing it by hand. Anxiety thrummed in him. He stared at the mirror. What could she possibly have been thinking?

Blood ran down his fingers and swirled in the sink.

Gibson stood out on the stone veranda at the back of his villa. From that point he had a breathtaking view of the ocean and the harbor in the distance. It was beautiful there early in the morning and at night when the stars filled the sky. Women he'd taken there had all been in awe of the sky and sea.

He sipped champagne and stood there in the clothes he'd worn last night. He'd fallen asleep in the chair in his office, watching some of his best performances and admiring his smooth skills while awaiting word from Roylston.

For a time he'd been enraptured by his performances. Audiences loved him and clamored to know how he did his magic. At least that was what they said. In truth, and Gibson knew this was the truth, they didn't want to know how he did those amazing feats. They wanted to believe. No one did it better. Not Copperfield, not even Houdini himself.

The gold coin twinkled in the morning sunlight as Gibson rolled it across his knuckles. Magic had been his salvation. He'd found it as a child, watching performers and learning their tricks. Nothing about the rest of his life had satisfied him, not the riches, not the cars, not even the women.

Not until he'd learned how to kill. That was the greatest trick of all: the disappearance of another's life. He still didn't know where a person went when they vanished on the other side of death.

He'd been fifteen years old when he'd first killed. The nineteen-year-old girl he'd been dating had told him she was pregnant, obviously planning to burrow her way into the family money because she'd figured out who he really was and had come after him. She'd surprised him with her announcement, telling him while they'd been in a hot tub in a rented hotel room they'd gotten with his father's money.

Gibson had lost control then. At first. He'd clamped his hands around her neck and shoved her under the water. She'd screamed, but her screams had only come out as bubbles that made no sound. She'd fought, and she'd carved furrows down his arms. The scars were still there, grayed out over the years, but reminders all the same. Now he didn't think of them as scars. They were badges, commemorations of his performance.

After a time, too short a time, she'd stopped thrashing and had lain quietly, almost floating. The water had stilled, and he'd studied her face, so slack, so surprised. The blood from the cuts along his forearms had threaded the water with streams of scarlet fog.

That was where he'd been when his father's security people found him after he'd called his father. Years of therapy had followed, but Gibson had worked on his magic in those places, teaching himself more and more. He'd even taught himself to hide his bloodlust from trained observers till he was finally discharged from their care. Everything was illusion.

The girl whose life he'd taken was still presumed a runaway. That had been over a quarter century ago. His father knew how to make things disappear, as well. Gibson had to give the old man that. He respected that. But there was nothing his father cherished about him except the fact that he was the old man's only child and he knew it.

A sailboat ran with the wind out on the horizon, the white sails bright against the gray-green sea and the azure sky. Out on that boat, people would be partying. Probably there would be young people, young women.

The dark hunger stirred restlessly inside Gibson's belly and wormed up to his heart. He embraced the hunger and felt it blossom inside him. Little more than a week had passed since he'd last killed. Normally he didn't feel the need to take a life again so quickly.

But things had changed when he'd killed the woman detective in Atlanta. She had been so smug, so sure of herself, when she'd finally gotten him on the phone. She'd told him that she wanted him to come in for questioning, and Gibson had known she'd thought herself somehow clever enough to trip him up.

She'd been stupid. Gibson's father had tried to break him over the years, and the old man hadn't managed that, either. If he couldn't do it, no one else could.

That woman had been surprised, too, when he'd caught up with her. She'd been alone in her house. Her husband and their two sons had been at a baseball game. A cop's salary didn't provide much in the way of a security system, and her husband didn't make much more than she did. Gibson had been getting past security systems much more sophisticated for years.

He'd arrived at her house shortly after the husband and children had gone. After he'd stolen her away, he'd had hours to kill her in the rented hotel room, and he'd taken his time.

He closed his eyes and remembered, and the salt air around him reminded him of the stink of her blood. He hadn't been able to hear her scream the way he had some of his other victims. There had been too many close neighbors. He'd been forced to cut out her vocal cords first.

Gibson relished the memory, knowing it would

always be his. Then the morning heat on his face took him away from that time and brought him back to the veranda.

He realized he was no longer alone.

Turning, he found Roylston standing there with a tube in one hand. The man looked somewhat fatigued from staying up all night.

Gibson sipped the champagne. "Well?"

"The cop's not at his hotel."

The news irritated Gibson. After last night's debacle and the calls from the police about Sisco, he'd hoped to at last put an end to Heath Sawyer's threats. He'd called the man to distract him while Roylston and his team closed in on him.

"You're sure?"

"Yes. We broke into the room and took a look around. We found this." Roylston opened the tube he carried and pulled out a rolled poster. When he spread it, Gibson saw the photographs of the women he'd killed on display there.

Of course, not all of the women were there. Only a small sampling of those whose lives he'd vanished were represented there. Heath Sawyer and his dead partner hadn't figured out everything. Gibson hadn't started sending the White

Rabbit cards until the past few years. Just to make the trick more interesting and to build an audience.

"Then where is he?"

Roylston shook his head. "I don't know. His car was there, too. We found it in the parking lot. He's not driving it."

Heath's disappearance irritated Gibson. The man was a loose cannon. Gibson didn't think Heath could do anything to him other than make life somewhat uncomfortable, but he wanted the man out of the way at this point. "Did you trace the van he used last night?"

"We did, but we didn't have any more luck than the police did. The van has been used in some criminal activities before. Tracked its VIN number to some impounds regarding drug deals and theft, nothing else. It's a scab vehicle. Somebody rented it or sold it to the cop off the books."

"Then find that person."

"We're looking."

Gibson felt like exploding at Roylston, but he knew it wouldn't do any good. The man would only point out that killing the woman detective had caused all their current grief. And that maybe attacking the last woman so close to home hadn't been smart. He'd already mentioned those things. Gibson didn't want a replay.

He turned his back on Roylston. "Let me know when you find Sawyer. And put that poster in my office. I want to keep it. It'll make a fine souvenir."

Roylston stood there for a moment, and Gibson knew the man was angry. The cop had shown him up last night by getting away. Roylston wasn't used to being outfoxed. As much as anything, the man's professional pride was going to keep him tracking the Atlanta detective, and he wouldn't rest until he was in the ground or at the bottom of the ocean.

"Sure." Roylston walked away, his footsteps receding until they were covered over by the sounds of the surf.

Over the past few years they'd been together, Gibson had wondered if the day would come that Roylston would leave. After all, the man had helped cover up some of the murders over those years. He or his team had found the bodies Gibson had left behind and disposed of them. That was one of the primary reasons Gibson had started mailing in the White Rabbit cards. He'd wanted to claim his kills, to have people see those performances.

In the end, though, Gibson knew Roylston wouldn't leave. He'd stay, not out of loyalty, but because Gibson's father paid him well enough to stay no matter what Gibson did.

Gibson drained his glass and embraced the restless hunger that grew larger inside him. He would kill again.

Soon.

Chapter 14

Lauren held her bag of purchases in one hand while she used the key card with the other. The locking mechanism *thunked* inside the door, and the light cycled green. She pushed the door open and found Heath Sawyer standing at the vanity sink with his wet shirt in one hand and the big revolver in the other. His face was hard and cold.

His voice was a growl when he spoke. He lowered the revolver to his side. "Where have you been?"

Squelching the angry retort that sailed to the tip of her tongue, Lauren entered the room and allowed the door to close behind her. "I left a note."

"You shouldn't have left this room."

"We needed some things." She walked past him to the table on the other side of the room. "No, let me rephrase that—*you* needed some things. I went out to take care of it while you were sleeping."

"You could have woken me up!"

Lauren looked at the gun meaningfully. "Waking you might not have been the safest thing to do." She couldn't believe she'd felt so safe in his arms last night. Right now he looked cold and distant.

"Going out there by yourself was stupid."

Hurt and angry, Lauren looked at him and folded her arms. "Waking you so you could accompany me in that shirt would have been even more stupid."

Glumly, he looked at the sodden mess in his knuckled fist. The cloth dripped onto the carpet.

"Wash that shirt all you want. That blood's not coming out of that material. Or those pants."

Heath grimaced. "This is only the third time I've washed it. It's getting cleaner."

"With all the blood and the wrinkles you're going to have, you're going to look like an accident victim. You'll draw attention, and I don't think you want that." Lauren reached into the shopping bag and took out a pale blue light-weight long-sleeved, tapered dress shirt, khaki slacks, underwear and socks. She tossed the clothing to Heath, who dropped the soaked shirt in the sink and managed to catch everything. "I got you a matching jacket, as well."

"Suits aren't really my thing."

"I could tell that by the suit you wore to Megan's funeral. If those guys come hunting us again, you should look different. I thought maybe something more upscale might work. I have clothing that doesn't scream beach bunny."

"I kind of liked the orange-and-white bikini."

Feeling her cheeks flame with embarrassment, but pleased that he had noticed, Lauren tried to ignore him. She gestured at another bag. "I also picked up shoes and a belt. They were all out of gun holsters, so you'll have to make do."

A brief grin flickered in those green-flecked gold eyes. "Sounds expensive."

"It was. You're going to pay me back." She stared at his chest, at the interesting scar on his side, and made herself turn away from him. "Go shower. I also brought breakfast."

For a moment, she thought he was going to argue, but she heard him pad away. The bathroom door closed. After a few minutes, during which she couldn't help imagining him taking his clothes off and what the sleek lines of his body would look like, the shower came on, and she knew everything she'd imagined was about to turn glistening wet.

Then she remembered the bag of toiletries she'd picked up for him, too. She knew delivering them to him could wait, but she couldn't help picking up the small bag and going to the bathroom door. She hesitated a moment, then knocked.

"Yeah?" Heath's voice rose over the sound of the shower.

"I forgot. I got you a razor, some shaving cream and a few other things you might need."

He didn't say anything.

"I can leave them out here, or I can open the door enough to put them in the room."

"Put them in the room."

Opening the door just a few inches, resisting the urge to peer around the door, she reached into the room and placed the bag on the sink.

Although she didn't look toward the shower, the mirror and the angle gave her a good view.

The translucent shower curtain only softened the hard planes of his body a little. On the other side of the barrier, Heath looked nude, but he didn't look naked. The room smelled of soap, and the air was thick with humidity. Steeling herself, Lauren withdrew.

She sighed in frustration, returned to the table, and focused on the bag containing the breakfast she'd picked up at the market. Detective Heath Sawyer was just too attractive for her own good.

Heath stood under the heated spray of the shower and wondered what he'd gotten himself into. *She's not your partner. She's a civilian. You're letting her get in harm's way.* Jackson's words haunted him.

He ducked his head under the spray and told himself that he didn't have a choice. He wasn't putting her there. She was putting herself there. All he could try to do was keep her alive.

He kept thinking about how she looked. Those khaki pants she'd worn hugged her hips, and that orange top was on the verge of driving him crazy. Her clothing wasn't revealing, was tasteful, but it showed off just enough of her body that he wanted to see the rest of it.

He growled at himself and turned the water on cold full blast, till all he could think about was the cold. He almost froze to death before he could get those kinds of thoughts of her out of his mind.

After drying off, he wrapped a towel around his waist and stepped in front of the sink. The small bag of toiletries sat to one side. He fished out the shaving cream and razor first, then lathered up and managed to scrape his face smooth without nicking anything.

She'd bought deodorant, facial cleansing soap, toothpaste and toothbrush, mouthwash and a few other things. Heath didn't know what all of it was, but Jackson Portman would. The man was a metrosexual to the nth degree. Guys who got on the wrong side of him were often surprised by how nasty he could be in a dustup.

Heath administered what he could figure out, then dropped the towel and got dressed. He looked a lot different when he was finished. Once he transferred all of his personal effects from his cast-off clothing to his new clothes, he bundled up the pants and socks and stepped out of the bathroom.

Lauren wasn't in the room. She was at the table on the balcony that overlooked the harbor. She'd changed clothing, too, evidently in the room while he'd been in the bathroom showering, and that definitely stirred thoughts in his mind. She now wore a dark orange ruffled sundress with spaghetti straps that hit her midthigh.

The balcony was tiny, hardly tourist-worthy, but it held a small round table and two chairs under a faded umbrella decorated with seahorses. All of the red ones had bleached out to a dirty gray, but enough of the color remained to show what they had been.

"That may not be safe out there." Heath picked up the soaked shirt and added it to his pile of discards, rolling it in the center and putting it in one of the empty plastic bags.

"If anyone is looking for us, they didn't find us so far. I don't think they're going to find us this morning."

"You don't know that."

"I'm not eating breakfast in that room."

Heath pulled on socks, then stepped into a pair of brown shoes that went well with the pants. He added the slim belt and picked up the .357 on his way to the balcony.

The table held a selection of foods in cartons. He recognized the pineapple and watermelon and bananas and breadfruit. He'd had the ball-shaped fried dumplings before, and he knew that the other two servings held meat. There was also a small pot of coffee from the room's coffee-maker and a carafe of orange juice. He picked up a plastic fork and one of the disposable plates.

"What's this?" He pointed at the yellow clumps in one carton.

"Ackee and saltfish. Ackee is a fruit. Very subtle flavor that complements the salted cod."

"You've had it before?"

"I have. Not everything has to be steak and potatoes."

"I look like a steak and potatoes guy to you?"

She wore large sunglasses, so he couldn't see her eyes, but her lips quirked up at the corners. "You do."

"Okay. What's this?" Heath pointed to the carton that held what looked like fish and tomatoes.

"Sweet and sour fish. Mackerel sautéed with onions and tomatoes. I picked all of this up at the Pegasus Hotel."

"I'm paying for breakfast, too?"

"No. *I'm* buying breakfast." The sunglasses centered on him. "You saved my life last night."

"I think we actually saved each other's life." Heath pointed his fork at the cartons. "You want to divvy?"

"I thought you were old enough to feed yourself."

"When somebody lays out a spread like this, I get intimidated." Heath rolled up his sleeves while she sorted out the cartons. "Manners aren't my strong suit. Maybe you could have guessed that, too."

"You look good in those clothes."

"Thank you." Heath felt a little self-conscious at the compliment. He knew he turned women's heads every now and again, but they didn't compliment him on the way he was dressed. His eyes, his hands, those were the usual things. "You look good, too. How did you get the sizes right?"

"The shirt was easy. I just checked the shirt

you'd been wearing. I did the same for the shoes. The pants were a guess."

"You guess pretty good."

"I help outfit a lot of stage magicians. Extra pockets. Hideouts. Things like that. I have to know sizes and what you can do with them." She finished putting food on her plate.

Heath looked around and smiled. "You've got the view. The table. The food." He tapped the fork against the empty plastic flower vase glued to the table. "I'm surprised you didn't get a table setting, too."

With a small grin, she spread her hands, and a bright pink hibiscus appeared in them. She stuck the flower stem into the neck of the vase, and it sat there.

"Now you're showing off." Heath frowned at the flower. "How did you manage that?"

"The flower?" She looked terribly innocent.

"Yes, the flower."

She shrugged. "Magic. Don't you believe in magic?"

"No."

"Maybe you should start." She picked up her fork and speared a pineapple chunk.

"You are missing a candle, you know?"

An arched eyebrow rose above the sunglasses lens. "You believe in candlelight dinners?"

"I do. Easier to believe in than magic. And you can have steak and potatoes by candlelight. Does that surprise you?"

"What do you think?"

Heath forked a helping of ackee and saltfish into his mouth and chewed. It was surprisingly good. "Actually, I don't think you get surprised by a lot."

She didn't say anything, just kept eating for a moment. Then her expression sobered. "What are we doing after breakfast?"

Heath hated that the casual flirting had been set aside. It was easy to believe, just for a little while, that he was in the Caribbean with a beautiful woman that might be the least bit interested in him. More than that, it was a pleasant diversion from the dark thoughts that had plagued him for the past few weeks since Janet's death.

"After breakfast we're going to my hotel room."

"That could be dangerous if Gibson's people are watching your room."

"Let's hope I see them before they see me. I have equipment there that I can use."

"It might be safer to get more somewhere else."

Heath shook his head. "My files are there, too."

The two men watching Heath's room weren't any of the bodyguards from the villa, but they weren't Kingston policemen, either. They were both African-American, decked out in casual wear and likely carrying concealed weapons. Judging from the tattoos and the scars and the way they manned their positions, they had military backgrounds.

Even though she wasn't trained for such things, Lauren was used to watching people and figuring out what they were about. Living in foster homes had taught her that, and everything she had learned told her these men were dangerous.

She sorted through the tourist brochures hanging on one wall, selected a few, then walked back out of the hotel. Heath, dressed in the lightweight jacket and amber-tinted sunglasses, waited in her rental in the parking area adjacent to the hotel. He reached across and opened her door.

Lauren climbed in and sat, pulling the door closed. "Someone's watching, but they're not any of Gibson's regular bodyguards. From the looks of them, they're military."

Heath's eyes narrowed. "What is it with Gibson and these military guys? There has to be some connection."

Lauren shook her head. "I don't know. Like I told you before, Gibson is almost a nonentity in the magic circles. He just…appeared, and he vanishes whenever he wants to."

"I know. Janet and I tried tracking him back through taxes, but all we ever reached was a legal firm that backed us off. We never got enough evidence to get a warrant to leverage the attorneys."

"What about the attorneys? Do they have access to people like Roylston, Sisco and the others?"

Heath looked at her in surprise. "Janet and I never thought to ask about that."

"Might be worth it."

Heath nodded and used the cell phone he'd purchased after leaving Lauren's hotel this morning. Lauren kept watch on their surroundings while he talked.

"Hey. Do me a favor. In the White Rabbit file on my computer, there's a listing for the attorneys Janet and I tracked Gibson back to. Run a background check on those people, see if you turn up any ex-military or paramilitary connections." Heath folded the phone and put it away. He looked up at the hotel.

"What are you thinking?"

"That my hotel room didn't have any alarms on the windows."

Looking out her window, Lauren spotted the fire escape snaking up the side of the building. "That's not a good idea. If there are people watching the lobby, you can bet there's someone watching the room."

"Yeah. From the outside. I'm not going in from the outside." Heath slid the revolver from under the seat and tucked it into the back of his pants. "Keep a lookout here. If you see something suspicious, call me on my cell."

Worry knotted in Lauren's stomach, but she knew better than to argue. It would only be wasted breath. "Good luck."

Heath left the vehicle, and Lauren slid over behind the steering wheel. She watched as he walked to the rear of the hotel and started up the fire escape. Keeping an eye on Heath and the front door of the hotel was hard, but she managed.

Chapter 15

At the fourth floor landing on the fire escape, Heath paused and hunkered down. He peered through the sliding door, unable to see through the drapes.

Drawing back an arm, maneuvering so his back was to the sliding door, Heath thrust his elbow into the glass and broke it. Turning back around, he used his jacket so he wouldn't leave fingerprints on the pieces and plucked out enough fragments to allow him to stick his hand through. Again using the jacket, he unlatched the door, opened it and strode through with the .357 in his hand.

His clothing lay strewn all over the room. The drawers were pulled out and dumped onto the floor. Someone had taken the poster of evidence. He cursed the theft and walked to the table where his gear was. The travel bag containing spare rounds for the revolver, restraints and other gear sat open under the table. His computer was gone.

A maid stepped out of the bathroom carrying folded towels. She wore earbuds that connected to an MP3 player hanging around her neck. Her black hair was pulled back in a ponytail, her skin was dark and she looked as if she was in her mid- to late twenties. The maid's outfit didn't flatter, but she had a hard, lean body.

"Oh. Sorry." The woman spoke with an accent. "I didn't think anyone was here."

Heath started to reassure her that he meant no harm, then he realized she was carrying folded towels *out* of the bathroom, not into. More than that, she was supposedly cleaning a room that looked as though it had been burglarized.

He reached for the gun, sweeping it up as she fired a pistol of her own from under the towels. Bullets whipped by Heath and jerked at the curtain folds. The sliding glass door shattered and fragments tinkled against the floor. There were no gunshots, only liquid *thwips* that told him she was using a silencer.

Throwing himself sideways onto the bed, Heath fired twice. The shots sounded incredibly loud inside the room, and he knew they were going to be joined in seconds.

The woman staggered back, dropping the towels and the pistol. She leaned back against the wall beside the bathroom and bit her lower lip in pain. Her left hand covered her right shoulder. Blood soaked into her blouse.

Holding the .357 on the woman, Heath engaged the secondary locks on the door. He walked toward the woman. "Who are you?"

She glared at him, eyes narrowing. "Room service."

"Tell me one that'll make me laugh or I'll put another bullet in you." Heath reached for the MP3 player, held it in one hand, and managed to stick one of the earbuds into his ear.

Men's voices carried over the frequency, not music. "That was a heavy-caliber pistol."

"That woman had a silenced nine, man. That's not her."

"On my way up. You watch the lobby."

"I will. If you see our target, give me a yell. I'll cover your six."

Heath pocketed the radio in his jacket pocket. "We don't have a lot of time to get to know each other, and my dance card looks pretty full, so I'm going to ask you one more time. Who are you?"

She shook her head. "Nobody you would know. I was contracted to kill you."

"By who?"

"By the man I work for. I don't ask questions. He pays me not to ask questions."

"Do you know Roylston?"

"I don't know anybody by that name."

"Let me see your arm."

Reluctantly, the woman lifted her hand. The bullet had hit her in the shoulder, sliding in under the clavicle and over the top of the scapula. She had some rehab ahead of her, but she wasn't in any serious danger of bleeding to death.

Taking advantage of his distraction, the woman attempted to knee him. Heath blocked her with his own knee and shoved her back hard enough to bounce her off the wall. He screwed the .357's barrel into the side of her neck. "Don't."

She froze, mouth hard and set, her eyes fluttering as if she expected him to pull the trigger at any moment.

Heath reached down for one of the towels and draped it over her injured shoulder. "Keep the pressure on to stop the bleeding. Have your friends get you to a hospital."

The woman hesitated, then nodded. "Thanks." She was a total professional.

Heath picked up her pistol by the barrel, dumped it into the equipment bag, zipped it up and hoisted the bag over his shoulder as he sprinted for the fire escape.

Even with the window rolled down, Lauren only thought she heard gunshots. It wasn't until people started running out of the hotel lobby that she had confirmation. She turned on the ignition, listened to the motor catch and glanced anxiously at the fire escape. She wasn't sure what she was going to do if Heath didn't appear there soon.

But he did.

He came out of the room and rapidly descended the stairs two and three at a time at a headlong pace that threatened to throw him off balance. By the time Heath reached the second floor, a man stepped out of the fourth floor room brandishing a large pistol. Lauren recognized him immediately as one of the two men she'd spotted in the lobby.

Leaning over the fire escape railing, the man fired three shots at Heath. The bullets ricocheted from the metal fire escape and from the hotel wall. The *spang* of metal on metal rang loudly. Heath threw himself over the second-floor landing and dropped the final story to the pavement, catching himself on one hand and bent knees. Turning, he brought his gun up and fired four times.

The return fire struck the fire escape around the gunman on the fourth floor, causing him to duck back to cover.

Lauren put the car in gear and sped closer to Heath, throwing open the passenger door. Heath tossed the bag into the backseat and climbed into the vehicle. He flicked the revolver open, shook out the empties, and started feeding new cartridges into the cylinder.

"Go! Now!" His gaze roved the street as Lauren wheeled the car in a tight turn and headed for the street. She floored the accelerator and held on to the steering wheel, hoping no one stepped out in front of her and a lane was clear in the street when she arrived there.

Bullets hammered the pavement around them. One cored through the roof of the car and knocked a hole in the floor next to Lauren's left foot. Another round took out the back glass. Then she turned hard right, screeching out onto the street. The car fishtailed wildly, and she fought the wheel.

"Straighten it out! Straighten it out!" Heath's hand flashed out and covered hers, holding the steering wheel tight. "Hold steady! Get the car under control first! Just like you would on slick ice!"

Lauren didn't know how he could speak so calmly. She wanted to scream, but she didn't have the time. The comparison to ice locked in for her, though. She was used to Chicago winters, and sometimes the streets felt the same way this out-of-control slalom felt. She stopped fighting the wheel and the car settled into place.

"Good. That's it."

Heath wasn't even looking at her. His attention was riveted on the street.

"What are you doing?"

"Guys set up like that will have a chase car set up, too, if they wanted to seriously cover the hotel. I want to find it before it finds us."

Lauren glanced in the rearview mirror and saw a dark sedan roaring up behind them, dodging in and out of traffic. "There it is! Behind us!"

"These guys are good." Heath turned in the seat and brought the pistol up in both hands over the car seat. "Cover your ear if you can. This is going to get loud."

Taking her right hand from the steering wheel, Lauren covered her right ear and waited tensely, grateful that the traffic in front of her was light. She pulled to the left, dodging around a Jeep, then popped back into the correct lane just as a cargo van rushed at her, horn blaring.

Glancing back in the rearview mirror, she saw the chase car was closing on them. Her heart thudded painfully, and she willed the car to go faster, but the engine just didn't have any more to give.

Heath opened fire without warning. Six thunderous booms filled the car, and Lauren lost most of her hearing.

"Turn right." Heath was beside her, yelling into her ear, and still he sounded as if he was a long way off. "Head into town. We have to find a place to lose this car." He emptied his pistol again and started reloading.

Looking up into the rearview mirror again, Lauren saw that the chase car was falling back. Gray smoke billowed from under the hood and green fluid rained between the front tires.

A few blocks farther on, the adrenaline aftershock hit Lauren, and she thought for a moment she was going to be sick. But she kept breathing, kept forcing her way through it, and she gradually calmed down.

"Are you okay?" Heath was looking at her so she could partially read his lips. When he'd at first leaned in, she'd thought he was going to kiss her again, and she knew she would have welcomed that. It was disappointing when she realized he was just trying to talk to her.

"Yes. I'm fine. Are you all right?"

"I'm good. Keep driving. I'll give you directions."

"All right."

"In the meantime, I need you to call the rental agency and tell them your car has been stolen."

"What?" She shook her head. "The police will start looking for it."

"The police are already looking for it." Heath pointed at an alley. "There. Pull in there."

Obeying, Lauren drove the car into the alley. No one was around at the moment.

"Stop here."

She did, but she couldn't help looking back through the broken window, knowing that the police were going to drive up behind her at any moment. "We can't stay here."

Heath was already getting out. He paused to pick up the empty casings from his revolver, counting them silently—or maybe just too quietly to be heard through the deafness in her ears—till he was satisfied with the number. He slid them into a pocket and looked at her. "Get out."

Lauren got out.

"Walk to the end of the alley and flag down a taxi. Hold it till I get there."

Lauren started walking, almost up to a run in the short distance. She glanced around, afraid that a taxi wasn't going to be nearby, then she spotted one coming up the street. She waved a hand to flag down the driver. She turned to call out to Heath, but he was already headed in her direction. Behind him, the rental car suddenly sprouted flames underneath it.

"What did you do?"

Heath took her by the arm and walked down the street away from the mouth of the alley. "I cut the gas line and lit a match. I want that car to be as confusing as possible for the forensics team when they get here. Did you call the rental company?"

"No."

"Do it. Tell them you got up and went out to get your car while you were shopping at the Jubilee Market on Orange Street. You left the car near the park there. When you went back to get it, the car was gone." Heath helped her into the taxi and climbed in after her.

The young driver turned around and took one earbud out. "Where to, mon?"

"Jubilee Market."

"Sure, sure. Have you dere in just a minute, mon." The driver replaced the earbud, bobbed his head in time with the music and pulled out into traffic.

Heath continued talking calmly. "The police will probably want to talk to you. I know I would if I was investigating this mess. All you have to do is tell them the same story." He looked at her. "Can you do that?"

"Yes."

"If you can't, we're going to get busted. They can't do anything to us in the long run because they can't prove that we did anything wrong, but they can send us home." Heath paused. "Unless you're ready to go home."

"No."

Heath threw an arm around her and gave her a hug. The driver looked at them in the rearview mirror and smiled, then went back to his music.

"Do you have the car keys?"

Lauren was surprised that she'd thought to get them in all the excitement, but she had. She showed him the keys.

"You can't have those." Heath took them from her, then separated them from the ring and began dropping them out the open window as the taxi raced along the street and sirens sounded behind them.

The taxi driver let them out on Orange Street, and Heath walked with her for a short distance. "I'm going to be around, but I don't want our names entered on the same report, okay?"

Lauren nodded.

"You were here, shopping, alone."

"Then where are the things I've been buying?"

Heath pulled her to one side where a small group of street artists were selling paintings. "Buy from people like this." He pointed at a painting with seahorses and held up twenty dollars. "People that just take cash and don't do printout receipts. You're looking for vendors surrounded by a crowd of tourists. Make small purchases. Knickknacks. Don't buy big and don't spend a lot of money, and you won't even be remembered." He looked at her and smiled. "At least, not by these people."

"Are you flirting with me?" Lauren was surprised at how calm she felt moving through the tourist crowd jamming the market. And she understood about the buying, too. It was all misdirection for whatever audience they drew.

His grin grew bigger. "Maybe a little. Breaking the law and getting away with it kind of makes me reckless."

"I thought you were a law enforcer, not a lawbreaker."

"You don't know everything about me."

A young woman in island dress nodded, took his twenty dollars and handed him the seahorse painting. Heath gave it to Lauren, who took it and crossed over to another booth that was selling small, colorful purses. She bought one and kept moving.

"Do you have enough money?" Heath kept pace with her.

"Are you offering to give me more?"

"Well, I did get you shot at this morning."

"You still have to pay me for that suit, mister.

I don't want you claiming poverty later." Lauren moved quickly, seeking out other tables and wares.

Heath chuckled. "You're awfully calm."

"This is a performance. I do performances."

"Are you going to be okay with the police?"

Lauren stopped at a table that sold shell jewelry. She didn't know who she was going to give the necklace and bracelet to when she returned home, but she bought them anyway and quickly moved on. "They're not sending me home, I can tell you that." No matter what it took, no matter what she had to do or how many times she was going to have to risk her life, she wasn't going to let Gibson get away with killing Megan. That wasn't happening.

Chapter 16

Thirty-seven minutes later, Lauren sat on a bench in the shade while sipping a strawberry juice drink when Inspector Wallace Myton came strolling up in an ill-fitting suit. Two uniformed patrolmen trailed at his heels.

"Ah, Miss Cooper, I hear that you have suffered misfortune." The inspector was shorter than Lauren, in his early fifties, and had warm, coffee skin. The unmistakable accent of the island echoed in his speech. He was balding and kept the sides shaved to salt-and-pepper stubble, and his neat mustache matched the color. In spite of his small stature, he had a long neck that had always put Lauren in the mind of a turkey during her dealings with him. He wore a light blue suit.

"Inspector Myton." Lauren looked up at him. "I'm surprised to see you."

"Are you?" Myton tapped a cigarette against the back of his hand.

"I just called in about my car being stolen." Lauren's heart beat faster and she struggled to remain calm. *It's just a performance. If you blow this one, they're going to send you home, and Megan's killer may never be found.* Thinking about her sister steadied her, gave her purpose and direction. She wasn't going to fail. She refused.

"So I heard. The rental agency called the police department, you see."

"I thought you only worked homicide investigations."

"I do." The inspector put the cigarette between his lips, then lit it with a book of matches. He inhaled, then let out a long stream of smoke. "Sometimes I work very hard to *prevent* them."

"Are you here to take my report, because there isn't much to tell, actually. When I went to the parking lot with my purchases, my car was gone. So were my keys. They were in my purse."

"A tragedy."

"I'm just glad it wasn't my car. The rental company said they'll send me another one."

Myton waved at the bench. "May I sit?"

Lauren put some of the bags onto the ground and made a place for the inspector. The two patrolmen continued to stand nearby.

Myton sat and started poking around in the bags. "My wife often comes out here. She likes little things like these. They bring her joy, but I fear we are running out of places to put these things."

Lauren started to worry that she'd gone overboard in buying. Heath had helped, and they'd ended up with quite a haul.

The inspector looked at her. "I hadn't taken you for a collector of amateur arts and handcrafts."

"I'm not." Lauren smiled. *Performance.* "And I have a small apartment. Most of what you see here is going to be given to people I grew up with in foster homes. When you move around like that, you end up with a lot of brothers and sisters."

Myton smiled. "Yes, I suppose you would." He

gestured with his cigarette. "And you are close to these other brothers and sisters?"

"Yes."

"Like you were with Megan?"

Lauren let the smile disappear from her face. "No. Not as close as I was with Megan." She gave the inspector a hard look. "Why would you ask something like that?"

"Forgive me. Perhaps sometimes I am insensitive. I am a very inquisitive man. In part, it is what makes me good at my job."

Unable to reel in the anger that the inspector had ignited, Lauren lashed back. "If you're so good at your job, Inspector Myton, why haven't you found the person that killed my sister?"

"I have touched a nerve."

"Yes, you have."

Myton shrugged. "Such is the nature of this business that I do. Sometimes I must ask the hard questions. Like, would it surprise you to know that your stolen vehicle was involved in a shootout at a hotel only a short time ago and later burned in an alley?"

"After hearing how my sister died, I'm not

much surprised by anything these days." Lauren kept her face unreadable.

"Then you deny that you were involved?"

Lauren waved at the bags of purchases. "I've been shopping. I noticed the car was missing. I checked for my keys. They were also missing. I was told the market was notorious for pickpockets."

"So it is." Myton took another hit off his cigarette and expelled smoke. "These *thieves* who took your keys, I think they must have been very lucky to find your vehicle in all those that are parked around here."

"Not if they saw me leave it and decided to take my keys."

"So you were a prospect targeted by these people?"

"I don't know."

"Because I have to ask myself, why would a thief take your car, then go to a hotel and start shooting?"

"Maybe he didn't have cab fare."

Myton laughed at that, and the sound was genuine. He pointed his cigarette at her. "That is a very funny answer."

"Who was shot at?"

"Alas, that is also a question to which I do not have an answer at present. But soon, perhaps. I am still working on things." Myton stood and brushed ashes from his suit coat. "I am a very patient man, Miss Cooper. Eventually all answers come to me. I'll bid you good day, and I hope that your next experience with a rented vehicle goes much smoother than your first."

"Thank you."

Myton started to walk away, then he stopped and looked at her. "You know, you have never said what you are doing back in Kingston."

"Vacation."

"I would think, given the circumstances, there would be better places to vacation."

"Not at the moment."

Myton dropped his cigarette to the pavement and crushed it out underfoot. "Have you seen Detective Heath Sawyer since you've been back?"

Lauren thought about that for only a second. There was no right answer, and she thought it was better to go with the lie than an admission at this point. "No. Why?"

"Because he is still here, too. I thought it

wouldn't be too much to presume that the two of you might run into each other."

Lauren didn't say anything. A midsize car glided to a stop in front of the bench. The driver wore a cap that advertised the rental agency Lauren was using. He got out with a clipboard and searched the surroundings till he spotted Lauren.

"Miss Cooper." The driver smiled and waved the clipboard. "I have your car."

Lauren got up, grabbed some of the bags, and headed for the car. The driver opened the trunk, then scurried over to help her. Myton gestured to the two uniformed patrolmen. They stepped in and helped transfer purchases, as well.

Once she'd signed the rental form, the driver told her that he would take a taxi back to the agency. Myton came over to hold the door open to allow Lauren to slide behind the steering wheel, then he closed the door.

"Have a good day, Miss Cooper. Please be safe."

"Thank you, Inspector." Lauren put the car in gear and pulled into traffic. Her cell rang almost immediately.

"Hey." Heath's voice sounded laconic, as if

getting shot at and burning cars was an every-day thing. Maybe back in Atlanta it was.

"Hey." Lauren's clenched stomach relaxed a little when she heard him.

"Good performance. Very nice."

"So what do we do now?"

"Standard police work." Heath didn't sound happy about that. "We watch, we learn, we hope we catch a break. Gibson is rattled now. He's trying to manage his situation because I'm making him uncomfortable. With your help, though he doesn't know that. What I'd like to do is find out who the new players are and what they're doing here."

"You said you didn't recognize any of them."

"I didn't, but you're not the only one that can pick up things that don't belong to you. I picked up the weapon the *maid* used at the hotel. I'm going to run her fingerprints, see if we get a hit. She was an ice-cold pro. Somebody will know her."

"Do I need to circle around and pick you up?"

"No. I'm in the taxi four cars behind you."

Lauren glanced in the rearview mirror and counted back cars till she spotted the taxi.

Knowing he was there made her feel safer, not as alone.

"I'll meet you at your hotel. Wait for me in the lobby."

Heath sat at the desk in Lauren's hotel room and worked on the captured pistol. He'd gotten some mechanical pencil lead from the gift store in the hotel lobby, chopped it fine with a razor blade purchased from the same place, and turned it into a fine powder. A brush from a small cosmetic kit, also bought for an unconscionable price, allowed him to dust the graphite onto the pistol's surface.

The natural lighting from the balcony door provided plenty of illumination to see the latent friction ridges on the weapon. Using transparent tape, he lifted the prints, then affixed them to a sheet of typing paper that the gift shop had carried.

"Who knew the gift shop was one-stop shopping for your own CSI lab?" Lauren sat in the nearby wingback chair and watched the proceedings with avid interest.

Heath went in search of another print, this one

off the magazine. "A very pitiful excuse for a CSI lab."

"It seems to be getting the job done."

"I hope. And I hope she has a file."

Lauren kept working on her iPad. Heath didn't know what she was doing, but when she wasn't watching him, she was very intent on the device. She looked up again. "You're different than I expected."

"How so?" Carefully, Heath extracted one of the bullets from the magazine. When he dusted it, nothing came up. He hadn't expected to net any results because brass could get lost during a shooting. Keeping up with ejected casings could be too problematic. The woman had been a professional. She would have used gloves to load her weapon. Dusting the bullet had been to confirm his impression, and it had.

"I knew you were a tough cop. I could tell that from the first time I met you."

"During which time you were thinking I was a morgue attendant."

She frowned at him.

"Okay, maybe that's too soon. Blame it on tiredness."

"You slept later than I did."

"True."

"No, I knew you were tough."

"Had a lot of experience with tough cops, have you?"

A ghost of a smile turned up her lips, and for a moment he could see the little girl she might have been. "I grew up in foster care for half my life. Of course I knew tough cops."

"Any outstanding juvenile warrants?" Heath affixed another print to the paper. He had eight of them so far, which he thought was a good number.

"All of them have aged out, Detective."

"Then you're safe." Heath reached down into his equipment bag and took out the camera he'd brought with him. He took several hi-res photographs of the prints, then sent the images to Jackson Portman's email at the P.D. Whoever had broken into his hotel room had stolen his computer, but the camera was Wi-Fi capable. "So how am I different?"

"You're more thorough than I thought you would be. And you know a lot about your job."

"I have to know a lot about my job. It's what I

do." He looked at her while waiting for the up-loads to cycle. "How many coin tricks do you know?"

"Disappear? Appear? Change? What kind of coin?"

Heath grinned. "I guess neither of us learns just one trick, do we?"

"I suppose not."

Heath glanced at his watch. It was after two. "We missed lunch, and breakfast was too long ago. It's going to take my partner a while to run down these prints, if he's able to. Let's assume the restaurant in this hotel is adequate. Do we do room service or dine there?"

Lauren thought for just a moment. "Let's eat in the dining room."

The decision was disappointing. Heath enjoyed his time alone with Lauren, probably more than he should have. He stood, wiped the graphite from his hands and picked up his jacket.

She smiled at him. "It'll give you another chance to show off your new wardrobe."

"A limited wardrobe, it seems, since recovering my other clothing is going to require me talking to Inspector Myton and his people."

"Maybe you can go shopping with me this time."

"I'd rather have a root canal."

Only a few people were in the dining room when Lauren and Heath arrived. They took a booth in one corner and looked at the menu for a while.

Lauren didn't know what Heath was thinking. His face didn't give away much about what was going on inside his head. She watched him over the top of her menu, and for just a short time, she imagined what it might be like to actually be out for a meal with him.

He was attractive, and it wasn't just the physical aspect. Not just the tough cop, or even the thorough cop. He was...attentive. He watched things, really saw them. And he saw people, too. She knew that she aggravated him. He didn't like the fact that she didn't listen to him, but he respected it. When the situation was bad, he trusted her, too. Even when it was circumstances that he knew Lauren had never been involved with.

Not a lot of men would do that. Especially not

rugged, tough, thorough homicide detectives. She decided that maybe she'd been wrong about him in the beginning, except that she knew she was right. Under prevailing circumstances, Heath Sawyer could be a complete jerk. That was just how he'd been made. It was going to take a woman with a lot of patience to put up with him. Lauren had never been patient for anybody outside of herself and her family.

He looked up at her without warning, and their eyes met. He smiled inquisitively.

Lauren broke the awkward silence quickly. "What are you having?"

"They have steak. They have potatoes. I'm a happy guy."

She laid her menu aside. "Aren't you going to ask what I'm going to have?"

"Sure. What are you going to have?"

"Maybe you should guess."

"Nope."

"Why?"

"Because, even if I get it right, you'll just say that's not what you're having and tell me you're having something else."

Despite herself, Lauren grinned. She knew she would have done exactly that.

"This lady has been busy." Jackson Portman spoke over speaker function while Heath's phone sat on the desk. Lauren's iPad sat beside the phone. Jackson had sent his findings to a Dropbox account Heath had activated to receive the file.

Lauren sat beside Heath, but he was asking the questions. She stared at the hard-faced woman in the photo. The image had been captured in three-quarter profile. She'd been wearing combat fatigues and a helmet. She carried an assault rifle in her arms. Her eyes were dead and flat.

"Who is she?"

"Name's Suzana Veslin." Jackson spelled it out. "She's a mercenary. A high-end operator out of the Balkans. Interpol has conflicting reports about where she's from exactly. They believe she was sold into human trafficking and fought her way out with a toothpick. After that she learned how to use knives and guns. I have to tell you, amigo, you went up against this one and came out on top, you're better than I think you are or you got lucky."

"It's always good to be good, but it's better to be lucky."

Lauren couldn't believe Heath was passing off whatever had happened inside that hotel room so casually. A chill tightened her stomach at the thought that he had come so close to getting killed.

"Who's she working for?" Heath slid his fingers across the iPad, changing out the first image for others that showed Veslin in military gear in other places.

"Hard to tell, bro. Some of the big corporations have used her to get back hostages, but Interpol says she's been used on dark ops most of the time. She's taken hostages, killed people, all the bad stuff."

Heath reached the end of the images, then started over. "Doesn't make sense. A guy like Gibson wouldn't have access to people like this."

"You've gone up against his people." Jackson's voice was tense. "You can't deny what you've been dealing with. Veslin isn't quite to Roylston's pedigree, but she's close."

"Any connection between Roylston and Veslin?"

"None that I can find. None that Interpol and

a half dozen other international agencies know about. By the way, I'm getting some heavy interest from some of those people. They want to know why I'm asking."

"Tell them you're curious."

"Yeah, because that'll satisfy them."

Heath tapped the desktop irritably. "There's a connection somewhere. We just have to find it."

"I know. I'm looking. You guys just need to watch yourselves down there."

An hour later, Heath was cleaning both his weapons, the revolver he'd gotten and the 9 mm he'd picked up from Suzana Veslin, getting them ready to use. While he'd been doing that, he'd been watching Lauren. She sat cross-legged on the bed, fingers working intermittently on the iPad. She'd changed out of the sundress, much to Heath's chagrin, and into cargo shorts and a tunic top, which wasn't bad. She'd also pulled her hair back into a short ponytail. He admired the way she worked, full-blown concentration, no holding back. He wanted to ask her what she was working on, but that would have meant direct interaction and would have robbed him of the chance to watch her. When she moved, she was smooth and graceful, and he liked the curves and lean tautness of her body. She was made well. There was no other way to put it.

She looked up at him and caught him staring, almost like earlier in the dining room when he'd looked up from the menu and caught her looking at him. For just a moment, everything felt awkward. Then she smiled at him.

"Want to guess where Gibson is going to be tonight?"

That caught his attention, and the awkward moment fled. "Have you turned into a mind reader for real now?"

"No. But I know where he's going to be."

"Where?"

"Have you heard of Agony House?"

Heath thought for a moment and finally came up with it. "Some kind of haunted house?"

"Yes." Lauren's smile grew wider. "Supposedly a *very* haunted house with a long and bloody history. They're having a fundraiser there tonight for a children's nonprofit organization."

"Why do you think Gibson will be there?"

"Because I see it in the crystal ball." Lauren

turned her iPad around, showing him a Twitter page. She tapped one of the entries with her forefinger.

I'm gonna be at a haunted house 2nite with the Amazing Gibson! Check out Agony House!

A tiny url was provided after the announcement. Lauren tapped it and the iPad linked to a website dedicated to Agony House. In the center of the page was Gibson's photograph.

Chapter 17

At 8:00 p.m., Agony House was lit with baby spotlights that picked up the color from the ocean out front and the sky above that tinted the white exterior blue. The original house had been built in 1817 by a sugarcane plantation owner for his new bride, and that was only part of the story. Lauren had told Heath the rest of it while they'd gotten ready for the soiree, and he still couldn't believe everything he'd heard.

The house had been remodeled several times over the years, but in 1957, Prudy Cranmer, a small-time Hollywood actress who had married big-time money, purchased the estate. Several films had been shot there, most of them low-budget thrillers and a few horror movies.

The actress had left Agony House to her grand-daughter. These days Agony House continued to be, according to Lauren, a place of mysterious happenings and curiosity.

Heath stood in front of the hotel and felt dwarfed. Fountains sprayed up from a half dozen pools, three on either side of the wide stone steps that led up to the main lobby from the beachfront plaza. Several of the guests talked about the rumors of ghosts and offered testimony as to what they would do when they found one tonight.

Heath drifted in with the herd and paid the price of admission at the door. Lauren was already inside, and he felt uneasy without her in his sight. The past couple days had been filled with close calls. Tonight wouldn't be any different.

Inside the hotel, Heath found an alcove that allowed him to watch everything while staying somewhat in the background. Everyone had gathered in the main room to await the start of the show. At the bar set up in the corner, Heath paid for a bottled beer and returned to his post.

At 8:45, Lydia Cranmer, the granddaughter of

the actress who had initially purchased Agony House, put in her appearance. The lights were dimmed, and a baby spotlight dawned at the top of the long stairs. No one had been allowed access to the upper floor yet.

A hush fell over the crowd as they waited expectantly.

"Ladies and gentlemen, my name is Lydia Cranmer, and tonight you are my guests." She smiled at the crowd. "Welcome to my home. Welcome…to Agony House." She threw an arm theatrically into the air.

A laser light show suddenly erupted, and bright colors blazed around the ceiling. The kaleidoscope of neon lights whirled faster and became a blur.

Then they disappeared, and the lights went out, leaving the grand room doused in shadows. The blue light glowing outside created just enough illumination to allow people to see a few feet into the cottony darkness.

The crowd started whispering, wondering if this was part of the show. A few of the women grew scared, and a few of the men did, too. Heath was convinced it was all theater, but he was frustrated that he didn't know where Lauren was. He hadn't liked the separation aspect of the plan.

The baby spotlight came on again, and this time it picked up Lydia Cranmer halfway down the stairs, standing quietly at attention. "Many of you are first-time arrivals here at Agony House, and many of you are returning guests. It is good to see those of you who have returned, and I look forward to meeting new friends."

Gradually, the lights came back up, but they remained soft, a buttery-yellow that allowed deep shadows.

"The history of this house goes back to 1817, when plantation owner Benjamin Hervey built a magnificent home for his young bride, Abigail.

"Six months later, her husband was dead, and no one knew the cause. It didn't take long before talk of voodoo started every tongue wagging. When Abigail first came over to Jamaica, she'd suffered a dangerous fever that had been cured by a woman who practiced medicine. Her name was Tante Simone and she was reputed to be a *mambo,* a female voodoo priest.

"They say—though it was never proven—that

Tante Simone taught Abigail as much about the dark arts as she did about the healing ones. They say—though this, too, is disputed in legends and stories—that Abigail took her husband's life because he had taken her from her home and caused the drowning deaths of her family during an ocean voyage to visit Abigail."

Heath sipped his beer and watched the crowd.

"Eight years into Abigail's widowhood, a storm struck Agony House and caused massive damage. It looked like Abigail was going to lose her house because she couldn't afford to rebuild it. So she sought out a rich suitor named George Bascombe—seduced him through voodoo, some said—and brought him home. Repairing the house drained the man's wealth, and it was said Abigail stole Bascombe's life."

Lydia waved to the back of the hotel. "The graves of Abigail, her husbands and some of the slaves who died here have been relocated, but they still exist. During the day, or tonight, if you dare, you're welcome to visit the cemetery. Just don't take anything. No keepsakes or mementos." She paused. "You can never be sure of what might follow you home. There are reports, never verified, however, of visitors to Agony House that returned home and found they'd brought a ghost with them. The dead still live here among us, after all. Every now and again, they reveal themselves to us."

Inside the house, everyone was silent.

Even though Heath knew most of the story from Lauren's briefing earlier, he discovered he felt a little uneasy. He chalked the feeling up to knowing that Gibson was going to be there.

"Tonight, Agony House welcomes a most special guest." Lydia smiled at the crowd. "I know you've all heard of the Amazing Gibson, one of the foremost magicians in the world these days."

A few of the people surrounding the crowd started clapping, but Heath thought maybe they were hotel employees salted among the rest of the guests because they appeared to be sober and not cowed by the retelling of the legend. The other guests picked up the applause till the grand room vibrated with the thunder of it.

The lights went out again, then a detonation exploded sharply enough to make Heath's eardrums ache. A pall of gray fog rolled onto the top of the stairs. When the baby spotlight flared to life again, going almost nova in its intensity, the bright light hit the fog and turned it into a white cloud.

Then Gibson stepped through it, clad in his trademark black suit. He regarded the audience quietly, then held up his black-gloved hands. Putting his hands together, he moved them as if he was kneading dough. Something white appeared between his fingers and grew rapidly. His hands suddenly shot up high over his head and separated.

A white dove exploded from his hands and beat its wings frantically, causing the audience to duck before the bird flew through the main doors and between the hotel employees who held them open. The lights came on in the hotel so the bird could be more easily seen.

When the audience turned back to Gibson, he breathed flames into the space over their heads. Then his hands plucked unseen things from the air, and he tossed shining silver discs into the crowd. Gleefully, the audience grabbed the coins or chased them on the floor.

Heath knew without looking that they were the signature coins Lauren had told him about earlier, the ones with Gibson on one side and him vanished on the other.

Finished with his coin trick, Gibson spread his hands in invitation and nodded graciously.

Lydia climbed the stairs to join Gibson. "Ladies and gentlemen, tonight Gibson has graciously agreed to act as your host for the tour. He, too, knows much of the history of this house."

Gibson took her hand and kissed it, bowing slightly. "I know some of the house's history, but I don't know it all. You are the expert in that area, dear lady. I am but a shadow from a passing flame." He turned over his hand, and suddenly he was holding a lit candle.

The audience clapped appreciatively as Gibson held the candle aloft briefly before handing it off to an assistant who stepped over to him.

Heath finished his beer and handed the bottle off to a passing server.

Lydia took Gibson's arm and waved to the audience to come up the stairs. "Come along. The original Agony House may be gone, but its memories live within these walls."

Hesitantly, then with growing speed, the audience followed.

* * *

Finally, at the end of the forty-five-minute-long tour, with Gibson doing sleight of hand tricks and extolling the history of the house, they ended up at the library.

"Come inside." Lydia waved to the group, urging them to step into the large room. "This is the most completely salvaged room in Agony House. The walls, the floor and the books were rescued from the original house and moved here, where they have stayed ever since. Several of our guests have often claimed to have seen Benjamin Hervey in this room."

A clutch of plush sofas occupied a baroque area rug in the center of the room. A writing desk sat to the left, on the opposite side of the room from the massive wall of books.

So far Gibson had given no indication of seeing Heath, and Heath believed that was because the man was so intent on soaking up the attention. The guy was definitely a glory hound around an audience, and that need for attention also explained the White Rabbit cards he mailed after the murders. Going into seclusion must have been hard on him.

Or maybe that was when he picked his next victim and prepared to deliver his next trick.

Gibson swung his arm to take in the room. "Imagine her, if you can, sitting in this room, locked away with stories of outlandish monsters and ghosts. Perhaps even a premature burial or two." His candle winked out and the room was shrouded in darkness.

An eerie female voice spoke in a heavy accent from one of the back corners of the library. "You don't have to imagine her in this room. You can hear her if you wish. If you have the nerve."

A chill crept up Heath's neck, and he had to check a shiver.

A small flame dawned in the corner and was reflected on the writing desk there. The desk faced the wall, and the light illuminated the figure sitting in the chair. She was dressed in a black mini-cocktail dress that showed off her figure, a hood over her head, and thigh-high black boots.

Heath's radar went off with a sonic boom inside him as he took in the trim figure, the legs encased in black lace stockings. Even though he had spent a lot of time with her the past couple days, it took him a moment to recognize the woman.

Lauren.

His mouth went dry at the sight of her, and he couldn't help staring. Then, somewhere in the dim recesses of his totally blown mind, he realized that they could both be in a lot of trouble.

Lauren tilted her head just enough for the candlelight to illuminate her mocking smile and left her eyes a mystery. "Do you wish to speak to Abigail?"

Lydia made her way to the tour group, which had evidently decided to keep a respectful distance. The candlelight managed to pick Gibson out of the crowd, as well. He looked like a malevolent shadow, and only the hard planes of his face stood revealed. His eyes were black pits above sharp cheekbones.

"I demand to know who you are." Lydia stood her ground, but she stood it a few feet away from Lauren.

"My name is Mistress Tereza." Heath couldn't believe the voice belonged to Lauren because it sounded so different.

"You're not supposed to be here. You're trespassing."

"No, I *am* supposed to be here. I was called by Abigail."

Hesitantly, Lydia turned to look at Gibson. The magician stood stock-still in the shadows and made no response.

Okay, she just blew his mind, too. Heath thought that was funny, but he was too anxious over the trouble Lauren might be in to enjoy the moment very much. But mostly he was drawn to Lauren, unable to decide if she was more sexy or more spooky.

"I'm going to call security." Lydia started to walk toward the door.

"If you do, you'll miss what Abigail came here tonight to say. You know that she talked to your grandmother, but has she ever talked with you? Would you forego that opportunity?"

Heath held his breath, knowing that Lauren had to be running a bluff.

Chapter 18

Lydia stopped at the library door, then walked back into the room. "All right, prove it."

Lauren spoke in a whisper. "Be careful challenging the spirits, Ms. Cranmer. Your grandmother warned you about such things. There are too many evil presences still associated with this house to risk their anger."

Face blanching a little, Lydia stepped back.

With every eye on her, Lauren walked to the coffee table in the middle of the room. She pointed to the sofa on the other side of her as she sat. "Please, sit. Together, Abigail and I will reveal to you that story."

Heath's breath was tight in his chest. He didn't know how Lauren was going to pull this off.

A few of the women in the tour group urged Lydia to sit when they saw that she was reluctant. Finally, probably more out of being a good hostess than anything else, she sat.

Lauren pulled two lighted candles from the air and set them at opposite sides of the coffee table. Heath knew the candles had to be the result of sleight-of-hand, but he hadn't seen them coming till they were there. She'd gotten his wallet without him knowing, though, so he knew she was good. Just not this good.

With the candles in place, Lauren looked at Lydia. "This knowledge isn't just coming from me, Ms. Cranmer. Abigail has touched those of your party. They have the answers, not me."

Drawn by the soft voice and the promise of a brush with the supernatural, the crowd hovered closer. Only Gibson, Roylston and Heath remained back, and the magician's attention was resting solely on Lauren.

"Do you remember when your grandmother told you she'd seen Abigail?" Lauren focused on Lydia.

"Yes."

"Good." Lauren waved an arm over the coffee table. Fire leaped from her fingertips for just a moment, blinding Heath for a second. When he blinked to clear his eyes, he saw that a small crystal ball had appeared on the table.

The audience murmured in appreciation and there was scattered applause.

"Please." Lauren looked at the crowd. "This is not a spectacle. Do not offend the spirits." She focused on one man in a loud Hawaiian shirt and khaki shorts. "You, sir, you know part of the date when Prudy Cranmer revealed to her granddaughter the conversation she had with Abigail. Tell me the month of your birth."

The man hesitated for just a moment. A stocky woman beside him slapped him on the arm. "Tell her, George." She turned to Lauren. "Oh, for Pete's sake, now you know what I have to deal with on anniversaries. His birthday is August ninth."

Lauren smiled and nodded her thanks. "August is the correct month, is it not, Ms. Cranmer?"

As if dazed, Lydia bobbed her head. "August, yes."

"But the ninth is not the correct day, is it?"

"No."

Heath kept an eye on Gibson, noticing the magician stood ramrod straight. Finally, he shook his head. "This is just cheap theater, Lydia. Don't buy into this."

Agitated, Lydia glanced back over her shoulder at him.

Gibson grinned and shook his head. "This is just a show. Vaudeville, nothing more."

"Is that what you truly believe?" Lauren locked eyes with the magician.

"Yes."

"So you do not believe in the spirits?"

Gibson grimaced and Heath wanted to grin. The magician had stepped right into that. "Of course I believe. I came here tonight to show these people the spirits that walk through this house."

"Then do so. Give me the date when Prudy Cranmer told her granddaughter of her visit from Abigail."

Shaking his head, Gibson grinned again, but there was no mirth in the expression. "You have the floor, *Mistress Tereza.* Why don't you do the honors?"

"Because I cannot do this thing without you." Lauren stood and held out her hand. "Take my hand."

Gibson held up his gloved hands. "I don't do that."

"Is there someone here that you trust?" Lauren turned a hand over toward Lydia. "Our hostess, perhaps?"

"No, I don't think so."

"There must be someone."

Gibson jerked a thumb over his shoulder at Roylston. "Him. Him, I trust."

"Very well." Lauren moved her hand over in Roylston's direction. "Take my hand."

The bodyguard looked at Gibson, who nodded. Gibson watched everything as Roylston took Lauren's hand. Heath tensed, thinking that the bodyguard or Gibson might recognize her from the other day, but she looked so different, and the lights were dim. Still, Heath's hand wasn't far from the gun holstered at his hip.

"Now, take Mr. Gibson's shoulder with your other hand."

A grimace twisted the magician's face. Obviously he preferred "The Amazing" to "Mr."

Roylston looked at his boss, and Gibson nodded again. Gingerly, the bodyguard rested his hand lightly on the magician's shoulder.

Lauren looked at Gibson. "I need you to first clear your mind. Empty it of everything."

Gibson looked impatient and gave a quick nod. "Mind's cleared."

"I do not think you have cleared your mind." Lauren continued looking at him. "I will ask Abigail to speak louder to you."

He shook his head. "You're not going to blame the failure of your little parlor trick on me."

"I will not fail because you will not fail Abigail. She will not allow it." Lauren turned back to Lydia with a small envelope in her hand. "Ms. Cranmer, please take this envelope. Inside is a card. Write down the date that your grandmother talked to you about Abigail's visit. Just the day, not the month."

Lydia reached into her clutch and took out a pen and wrote quickly.

"Please put the card back into the envelope and await further directions." Lauren turned to Gibson. "They say that you can touch the spirit world, that you too can know the unknowable. I only need access to your power for a moment."

Gibson didn't say anything.

Lauren handed him a card and envelope.

Gibson immediately took the card out and examined it. "It's blank."

"For now, yes, but you are going to write on it with your mind."

"I am?" Gibson smirked in disbelief.

"You and Abigail will write on the card."

"Okay, what am I supposed to do with it?"

"Hold it to your forehead and concentrate. Very hard. Use your abilities. You have the power. Talk to Abigail."

Gibson closed his eyes just for a moment while holding the card to his forehead. Then he opened the envelope and revealed the blank card. "I don't see anything written here."

"Patience. Trust the spirits. Everything is as it should be. Please give the card to this man." Lauren pointed to Roylston.

Gibson didn't move for a moment, and Heath

guessed that the magician was thinking of refusing. But the audience was watching him, putting him on the spot. He had to play his part. The performer in him demanded that. He handed the envelope to Roylston.

Lauren reached for the envelope, managing to get her thumb and forefinger on the envelope for just a moment before Gibson caught her wrist. The magician's grip hurt because pain flickered through her eyes for just a moment.

"I don't think so, Mistress Tereza. That envelope stays right there."

With a nod, Lauren released the envelope. "As you wish." She turned to Lydia. "Please use one of the candles and burn your envelope in the fireplace."

Lydia rose with the candle in one hand and the envelope in the other. The audience watched in quiet fascination. In a moment, the envelope was crumpled ash on the fireplace floor.

"Now, Ms. Cranmer, I need you to take the envelope from this man and take it to the coffee table."

Lydia walked over to join them. Roylston looked at Gibson, who nodded, then released the card. The magician followed the hostess to the coffee table.

Lauren walked to the fireplace and dabbed her finger in the black and gray ashes. She sat on the other side of the coffee table and looked at Lydia. "Open the envelope and lay the card on the table."

Lydia did.

Gibson smirked and waved at the card. "It's still blank."

Without a word, Lauren smeared the ashes across the card. "Blow the ash away, Ms. Cranmer."

Heath knew that Gibson realized he'd made a mistake. As careful as he'd been watching, he'd still been taken. He stood and walked through the crowd. Roylston and another man fell into step with him as they went out of the room.

"The sixteenth!" Lydia held the card up in amazement. "The sixteenth!"

Lauren spoke calmly. "Was that the day, Ms. Cranmer?"

"Yes. Oh, my, yes, it was." She looked at Lauren. "How did you know?"

Lauren shook her head. "I did not. Abigail did."

She smiled and touched the other woman's shoulder. "You have spirits that live here, harsh and unkind spirits, but you are under your grandmother's protection."

By the time Lauren returned to her hotel room, she'd partially come down from the nervous high from the performance, but her blood was still singing through her veins. She had noticed Gibson leaving the library at the end of the reveal. The man hadn't broken stride quitting the premises. That still made Lauren grin.

Chaos had erupted at the Agony House after that, and Lauren had demonstrated all the knowledge she'd picked up from the internet that afternoon. She'd always been a good student, able to absorb material quickly. Lydia Cranmer had been frazzled to a degree, gobsmacked by the "spirits talking," and—to a degree—devastated that Gibson had deserted her.

Heart still thumping, Lauren walked out onto the patio and looked out over the city. She hated being alone in her moment of glory. She and Heath had taken different cars from the Agony House to make sure they weren't followed. Heath had tailed her for a while to make sure no one showed any undue interest. When he'd been satisfied, he'd called her and told her to return to the hotel.

She'd expected him to follow her there. He hadn't.

Leaning on the balcony, Lauren thought about her performance. She'd always been reluctant to put on shows, though Morganstern and some of the other magicians who frequented the shop had urged her to. Megan had even begged her to try for one of the amateur nights in Chicago.

Always before, Lauren had told her sister, her mother, Morganstern and everyone else that she was satisfied selling magic supplies, that she didn't crave the limelight.

After tonight, Lauren knew that was a lie. She'd never felt more alive than in front of that impromptu audience in the Agony House library.

Someone knocked on the door.

Lauren crossed the room and peered through the peephole, spotting Heath out in the hallway. She opened the door and let him in. "Hey."

He smiled at her, looking at her from head to toe, taking in the costume she still wore. She'd forgotten she still had it on. "I have to say, I didn't expect this."

Lauren put on the accent again. "What? Mistress Tereza?"

"So who is this?"

Grinning, Lauren pirouetted. "This is a personality that I sometimes do in the magic shop. For private shows with friends. I told you, I like to do magic."

"You pack that everywhere you go?"

"Actually, I brought it in case I needed to change my appearance. I figured I'd break the pieces up and use them with other outfits. Mistress Tereza wasn't scheduled for an appearance."

"Good thing you brought it. You put Gibson in his place." Heath frowned. "You want to tell me how you pulled that off?"

"Which part?"

"Let's start with the envelope thing. You never touched the envelope."

"Correction, I touched it. With this." Lauren dug in one of the hidden pockets of the hood she wore and produced a bit of wire that looked like a folded paper clip. The loop was just big enough to fit over her thumb. In the center of it was a small numeral 16. "I touched the card hard enough while Roylston was holding it to indent the card enough to leave an imprint that the ashes could reveal. Like your fingerprint kit you made."

Heath nodded. "I never saw that wire."

"Neither did anyone else. I'm good at sleight-of-hand."

"My wallet and I know this. So how about the guy with the August birthday?"

"His wallet knows I know sleight of hand, as well, but he doesn't. I had to pick the pockets of seven guys before I found one that would work."

"I never saw you in the crowd."

"You weren't supposed to."

"If you'd been wearing this outfit, I would have noticed you."

"I wasn't wearing this outfit." Lauren sat on the edge of the bed while Heath took the wing-back chair. She couldn't help crossing her legs and watching the sharp attention Heath gave her. That pull that existed between them was back, and it was stronger than ever. She wanted him to come for her, and if he did, she wasn't going to turn him away.

"All right, how did you know the date?"

"That was from research I found on the internet. When she was a little girl, one of her favorite singers died on that date. Prudy Cranmer told Lydia Cranmer that maybe Elvis would come talk to her the way Abigail came and talked to her. That was in an interview with the both of them back then."

"August sixteenth?"

"August sixteenth, 1977."

Heath thought for a moment, then shook his head.

"Seriously? You don't remember when Elvis Presley died?"

"I wasn't even born then. Neither were you."

"My mom *loves* Elvis. Megan and I used to try to tease her about it, but she would never budge. When we got to be teenagers, we watched a few of his movies and the *'68 Comeback Special*. We got it then. Bad boy looks and rock and roll."

Heath showed her a perplexed grin. "I don't see you as an Elvis fan."

"Then what do you see me as?"

Caught off-guard by the question, Heath shook his head. "I don't know, Lauren. I've never met anyone like you. I think I know you, then you do something that I would have never thought you would do. Like tonight. You were incredible."

Lauren smiled at him. "Doesn't seem to have gotten us any closer to catching Gibson, though."

"You don't know that. Guys like Gibson, they're used to operating by their timetable. You took that away from him tonight. You stole his thunder. He's not used to that. Tonight could have been the crack that will trip him up somewhere along the way."

They were quiet for a moment.

Heath looked at his watch. "I should be going."

That surprised Lauren. "Where are you going to go? Your hotel room is a shambles. The police are probably looking for you to talk to you about that." She took a deep breath, discovering that the air in the room suddenly seemed thin. "You're safer staying here tonight."

"I know, but you may not be."

Smiling, feeling a little more certain of herself, Lauren got up from the bed and walked over to him. "I can take care of myself." She leaned in close and kissed him, felt the soft heat of his lips pressed against hers, his stubble raking her chin, then—as if by magic—she pulled him effortlessly to his feet and led him to the bed.

Once he was on the bed with her, there was no turning back. He was insatiable, and his hands roamed over her body, stripped away the Mistress Tereza outfit and ignited a heat in her she'd never before experienced.

She relished the weight of his body pressing hers down into the mattress, felt the hard certainty of his erection against her thigh. Gasping, longing, feeling her need growing stronger and stronger, she pushed his pants down over his hips. She grasped his erection in one hand while his lips pressed against hers and his fingers found the molten core of her sex.

He stroked her and teased her till she was shivering and thought she couldn't take any more. Then relief came, bursting the tension that had swelled up inside her. She shook and was lost in bliss. Then she opened her eyes and looked up to see him smiling down at her.

Rolling to her side, Lauren pushed him over, pausing only long enough to reach into the night-stand for the marital aid kit that came with the room. She unrolled a condom over him, taking her time with the task, massaging and grasping till she knew she had him on the edge of control.

She leaned down and kissed him, then looked into those green-flecked gold eyes as his senses spun into overload. "Not so calm now, are you?"

He didn't reply. He just pulled her over on top of him in an inarticulate growl. He slid in instantly and started trying to move. Lauren pressed her hands against his chest, stilling his movement. Then she began to ride, feeling his hard length fill her each time she rose up and sank back down. He struggled to hold back, but she knew he couldn't, and she gloried in her ability to drive him past the point of control. She felt his release, felt him go stiff, then relax.

She lay there, enjoying the feel of his body against her. She rubbed her hands over his shoulders, just wanting to be next to him. Instead, he lifted her up bodily and rolled her over onto her back again. Then he was driving into her, hard as ever, and this time the pace was relentless. Her senses shattered and spun and fell into a world she'd never before seen.

Chapter 19

The shrill ringing of Lauren's cell phone woke her the next morning. Snuggled up against Heath, she didn't want to answer it, but as soon as the cell quit, it started ringing again. Grudgingly, she rolled away from the warm man beside her, who still somehow managed to sleep blissfully unaware, and grabbed her phone from the night-stand.

"Hello." She glanced at the bedside clock and discovered it was 9:12 in the morning. Not many people had her personal cell number. She expected to hear her mom's voice.

"Tell me you are the Mistress Tereza that visited the Agony House last night."

"What?" It took Lauren a moment to place

Warren Morganstern's voice because she didn't think she'd ever heard the man that excited.

"Mistress Tereza. You know, spooky girl of magic and mystery. Your act."

"I don't have an act." Lauren sat up in bed, realized she was naked and felt self-conscious even talking over the phone. She pulled a sheet up to cover herself.

"Well, lady, you better get one together because I think you're going to need it."

"What are you talking about?"

"You worked the Agony House last night in Kingston, right?"

"I wouldn't say I worked it."

"I've seen the video. I'm saying you worked it."

"Wait. What video?"

"Somebody in the crowd was filming while you were supposedly channeling some ghost named Abigail. They uploaded the video to You-Tube. It's going viral, kiddo, and getting lots of attention. Piling up hits like you wouldn't believe. It's called 'Mistress Tereza at Agony House.' Some people are calling it 'Mistress Tereza Out Magics the Amazing Gibson.' Like I said, getting lots of attention. Professional magicians envy this kind of publicity."

Still not believing what she was hearing, Lauren climbed out of bed with the sheet wrapped around her. That, of course, woke Heath, and he gazed at her with sleepy interest. Even staying in bed till nine, neither of them had gotten much sleep. The night had consumed them.

She picked her iPad up from the desk, sat down in the chair, and brought up the YouTube website. She entered *Mistress Tereza,* thinking that would be enough, and found videos advertising things that she would never have done. Although some of them looked interesting enough to think about doing with Heath. She added Agony House and Jamaica, just to be on the safe side, to the search.

"Did you find it?" Morganstern sounded impatient.

"I did." In disbelief, Lauren watched her performance, split between seeing the video and reliving those moments last night. The residual rush she got from watching those events transpire filled her with excitement.

Heath sat up, reached for his pants and pulled them on, then padded over to join her.

"It's a great bit, kiddo. You remember Ernie Barber?"

"Yes. He's a booking agent for some of the magicians."

"Yeah, and he's already called me, wanting to know if I know who Mistress Tereza is. He's called a lot of people. Getting out there on the grapevine." Morganstern laughed. "I told him, sure, I know who she is. So he wants to meet. If this video continues to go viral. And Ernie and I both think it will because you pants Gibson in it. There's a lot of buzz behind this."

Lauren looked at the hit counter and couldn't believe the number she was seeing. "This many people have watched the video?"

"Yeah, it's great. Just goes to show you—you can be good all day, but none of it counts until you catch a break. You've been good for a while, you just haven't believed it. Looks like you're catching your break now." Morganstern paused. "So when are you coming home? This could be good for you."

"I don't do shows. You know that."

"Well, you did one last night, kiddo. I've watched it a dozen times this morning after one of the guys texted me about it. It's a good bit. Not terribly original, not flashy, but there's a lot of heart in the way you sold the story and that performance."

Yeah, that's because I was trying to get a chance to talk to Gibson, but that didn't work out well. She'd hoped to at least get an audience with the magician.

"Too bad you can't tweak Gibson's nose again." Morganstern chuckled. "*That* would be something to see."

The comment got Lauren to thinking, and she was certain Heath wasn't going to like it at all. "Can I ask a favor?"

"What?"

"I need some gear."

"What kind of gear?"

"Straitjacket. Escapology stuff. I'll send you a list."

"We gonna see Mistress Tereza again?"

Lauren watched the video play through again and saw areas that she could tighten up if she ever did it another time. "Yeah, I think you will."

Morganstern hesitated. "There's one thing, kiddo. The escapology is good, and I know you've been working on some stuff, and you're good with the straitjacket, but it's dangerous if you don't have a trained crew around you."

"I know. I'll be careful."

"Send me the list. I'll get it out to you post-haste. I gotta go. I gotta call some more people." Morganstern hung up.

Placing the iPad back on the table, Lauren looked up at Heath. He looked worried as he watched the YouTube video.

"That's from last night." He rubbed his stubbled jaw with a big hand.

"It is."

"So what's going on?"

"The video is going viral. Warren just told me it's getting a lot of notice in the magic community. Mostly because Gibson gets shown up in it."

He switched his attention to her. "So what's this equipment you're asking for?"

"An escape I've been working on. A riff on Houdini."

Heath frowned. "What?"

"Oh, it's something that's sure to get Gibson's attention, but you're not going to like it at all."

* * *

"I don't like this."

Two days later, Lauren climbed the mainmast of a motorsailer they'd rented for the stunt. The sun was bright and the ocean was relatively calm around them, rolling in gentle swells that lifted and lowered the boat. Festive balloons tied all over the rigging strained at their tethers and made the boat look like a flowering plant.

Connected through a radio channel, Heath stood on the beach two hundred yards away. He was near his usual observation spot to watch Gibson's villa. He watched Lauren through binocs and suffered through the churning of his stomach.

For the past two days, he had helped Lauren get the equipment ready, charter a boat and arrange for a film crew. In between those times, they'd constantly been in bed getting to know each other as lovers. Even now, staring at her in her Mistress Tereza outfit, all he could think about was getting her back into bed.

Except right now he was also thinking that she could get burned to death in the next few minutes. He really didn't like what Lauren was planning to do.

"Don't watch." Lauren sounded a little out of breath as she climbed the mast. "And Kadena loves this."

Kadena was the videographer Lauren had picked for the shoot. He was a young Jamaican who talked about himself in the third person and totally got on Heath's nerves. However, he was also a good videographer. Heath had liked his work.

"Yeah, well, Kadena isn't going to be swinging from the end of a rope in a straitjacket. He doesn't get a vote."

Lauren laughed. "It'll be fun. I've done this dozens of times. It's all about timing. I've just got to be out of the straitjacket before I run out of air."

"I might feel a little better if you'd told me you'd done it thousands of times."

"I only have to do it right once today."

Lauren sat on the yardarm of the mainmast for a moment. People on the shore and in the boats started snapping pictures. The young Jamaican sailor who had accompanied Lauren to the top of the mast started cinching her up in the straitjacket.

Feeling more and more uneasy by the minute, Heath swiveled the binocs toward Gibson's villa. He dialed in the magnification and spotted Gibson out on his veranda, dressed in black, his arms folded and not looking happy at all. Evidently someone had gotten word to him about the escape.

Shifting the binocs back to the motorsailer, Heath watched as Lauren, wrapped in the straitjacket, walked along the yardarm. Balancing itself was a feat. A bungee line was attached to her right ankle.

Several people in the boats and on the beach were pointing. They all recognized the straitjacket.

"Oh, my God! She jumped!" The speaker was female, but Heath didn't know who it was. He was watching Lauren plummet toward the water. She bounced four times before settling down into a low-hanging arc only a few feet above the sea level.

The Jamaican sailor who had strapped Lauren into the straitjacket leaned down over the bun-

gee cord with something in his hand. A heartbeat later, flames raced down the length of the
cord toward Lauren's bare legs.

Heath cursed. She hadn't told him about this
part of the act. "Lauren. *Lauren*."

She didn't respond.

Holding the binocs in one hand, Heath sprinted
for the motorboat he'd rented for the day. Even
with it, he knew he would arrive too late. Then,
just as the flames started twisting around Lauren's legs and black smoke trailed from the bungee cord, the tether that held her to the boat came
free and she dropped into the sea.

Clambering aboard the motorboat, Heath
cranked the engine over and accelerated away
from the beach. Only then did he realize the
ocean around the motorsailer was congested,
and he wasn't going to be able to get through
to Lauren. He yelled curses as he tried to bump
through the other vessels.

Long minutes passed as Heath watched helplessly. Then, finally, looking like a drowned cat,
Lauren surfaced. She waved to Kadena. A cheer
swelled up from the onlookers. Music chugged
from the motorsailer's onboard PA system, a

swirling and intense calypso grind infused with heavy metal. Several young people dove into the water and swam toward Lauren as she swam toward the motorsailer.

Heath relaxed, then grew tense again as police patrol boats arrived with whirling light bars and intermittent blasts of sirens. The other boaters were cheering and screaming in disbelief in a half dozen different languages.

Before Lauren could reach the motorsailer, a police boat powered up to her. A man threw out a life preserver and ordered her aboard. Heath cursed. The police were another thing they hadn't figured into their plan.

"What are you in for?"

Sitting with her back against the wall and her arms folded, Lauren stared at the bleak walls of the jail cell for a moment before turning to her bench mate and answering. "Setting myself on fire and jumping off a boat in a straitjacket."

The older woman sitting at the other end of the bench was heavyset, her head wrapped in colorful scarves. She stared at Lauren for a moment before speaking again, placing a hand over her heart. "It is a man what has done made you do these things, yes?"

Lauren smiled at that, still caught up in the adrenaline afterglow of pulling off the escape. "More or less."

"And you in love, too." The woman laughed. "I can done see it in your eyes. Girl, you are in a stewpot full of trouble."

A female jailer in a neatly ironed uniform stepped to the bars. She smiled a little. "If you ask me, I think what you did was pretty cool, but you done broke the law."

"I know."

"Someone posted bail for you." The jailer opened the door. "Come on. Time for you to go."

Lauren got up and stepped through the door. She didn't realize till she was in the hallway how restrained she'd felt in the cell. She also felt bad that Heath had arranged bail for her, though that was nice, too, because now Gibson would probably discover that they were working together.

The jailer led her to a back room and motioned to a small iron-barred security window where a gnarled man sat in a police uniform. Lauren hadn't had many personal effects when she'd gone into the water, only her driver's license. The man on the other side of the window had her sign for it, then slid it across in a manila envelope.

"Thank you."

The man nodded and pointed to the computer on his desk. The screen was turned so Lauren could see it. "That boy that shot your escape did a good job. Good thing, too, because you better not do that again in this city."

"I know."

The man shook his head and smiled. "Saw you at the Agony House, too. Quite the show, quite the show."

"Thank you." Lauren followed the jailer to the back of the building and ended up stepping through the door she was shown and out on the street where she and Heath had taken Sisco captive days ago. The sun was already going down. She'd been questioned and processed and kept waiting for hours. She'd begun to think that she would be spending the night in jail. She checked both sides of the street.

Heath Sawyer wasn't there waiting for her.

Roylston was. He was dressed in a nice suit

and wore wraparound sunglasses. "Mistress Tereza?" He looked at the phone in his massive hand. "Or should I say Ms. Lauren Cooper?"

Feeling a little frightened, Lauren focused on the man. The luxury car she had seen him driving Gibson around in sat at the curb. Another man in a suit, one she didn't know, stood beside the vehicle.

"Whichever suits."

Roylston smiled, and there was nothing pleasant or welcoming about the expression. "Gibson would like to meet you. If you're interested."

For only a heartbeat, Lauren hesitated. The plan was to entice Gibson with another video of Mistress Tereza, then meet him at their convenience. Not be swept away. She looked around the street again but didn't see Heath anywhere. She thought of Megan and how more proof was needed to name Gibson as her murderer.

No way was Lauren going to let Gibson walk on that.

No way.

She nodded. "Sure. I've been wanting to meet him. I wanted to tell him that night at Agony House, but he disappeared before I knew it."

"Gibson is like that."

"Maybe you could pick me up at my hotel in half an hour?" Lauren pulled at the outfit. "I smell like I took a bath in the ocean. I'd like a chance to clean up."

"Gibson is quite insistent about meeting you now. Don't worry about how you're dressed. There is a selection of clothing at the villa. Gibson often entertains guests. I'm sure you'll find something to wear."

Lauren still hesitated.

Roylston's smile faded a little. "I'm afraid the offer will expire. Gibson's time is very valuable."

Taking a breath, Lauren nodded. "All right. Let's go." As she approached the car, Roylston opened the rear door. When she got inside, the big man slid in beside her and closed the door.

The other man got in behind the wheel, put the car in gear and rolled into traffic.

Lauren craned her head over her shoulder and looked back at the street, still not seeing Heath.

"Expecting someone?" Roylston sat calmly beside her.

Turning back around, Lauren faced forward. "I thought maybe the media would be around."

"They're in front of the building. Gibson talked to someone in the police department and all parties concerned agreed that it would probably be best if you quietly disappeared."

Lauren didn't think the choice of words was by chance, and a shiver passed through her. She clamped down on the fear that prickled within her, trusting that Gibson wouldn't just spirit her away from the jail and kill her. Even he couldn't pull that off.

Chapter 20

Seated in a café across from the jail, Heath looked at the bail bondsman he'd recruited to get Lauren Cooper out of jail. "What do you mean she's gone?"

Denroy Paul was an earnest young man who hadn't quite escaped the laid-back attitude of the island. He was six feet tall and slim, his hair done in dreadlocks, and he had a very white smile that he liked to use a lot. He wore slacks and sandals and a white short-sleeved shirt.

"Just that, mon. I go there looking for this woman. I ask about her like I always do." Denroy shrugged. "Then the jailer, she tell me Lauren Cooper already be gone, mon. Someone else bailed her out." He grinned. "Must be you not the only one interested." He nodded. "I seen them videos, mon. Very good-looking woman."

Heath curbed the angry retort that landed at the tip of his tongue. "Did you find out who paid her bail?"

"Gibson. The mon who is the magician. You know him?"

"Not as well as I'd like to. How long ago did Gibson post her bail?"

Holding his forefinger and thumb an inch apart, Denroy shook his head. "Missed her by that much, mon."

Heath got up from the table. "I owe you anything?"

Denroy opened his hands. "Not me, mon. I didn't do nothing for you."

"Thanks." Heath hustled for the door, almost running by the time he got there.

Twenty-three minutes later, certain he'd violated every traffic law in Kingston, Heath pulled to a stop at his observation point on the beach up the road from Gibson's villa. A sand cloud ghosted gray around him, and campfires carved holes in the darkness that had settled over the beach. His heart ached when he thought of Lauren in Gibson's power.

During the whole drive, he couldn't help remembering Janet Hutchins and how he hadn't been there in time to save her from Gibson. That guilt had nearly eaten Heath alive over the past couple weeks. But he knew that he hadn't let Janet down. She hadn't had time to call for help when Gibson had gotten to her. She'd been gone before Heath had known.

He adjusted the binocs and swept the house. The luxury car's headlights dimmed in the circular driveway, then the dome light flared on. Heath's breath caught at the back of his throat as he watched Lauren step out of the car and walk up the steps leading to the house.

Standing at the window, fingers pulling the drapes slightly aside, Gibson stared down at his latest prey. She wore the same outfit she'd worn when she'd accosted the tour in the Agony House, only now she looked somewhat tawdry and bedraggled. She was still beautiful. There was no taking that away from her. Natural beauty always shone through.

His hunger to kill coiled like a dark thing at the back of his mind. He felt it sitting there, waiting to consume his senses when the time came. This time the hunger felt different, more alive and vital than it had before. It felt stronger, so much like it had felt the night he had killed the woman detective.

Only this felt much more pleasurable. The anticipation was almost sexual, and the desire turned physical.

She had offended him. She had seized the limelight that was supposed to have been his at the Agony House. The tour had been his to direct that night, and she had derailed his efforts.

And now, today…

He turned from the window and glared at the large computer screen on the inlaid desk that anchored his private sanctorum. The YouTube video of *Mistress Tereza* was frozen at the point that the woman was entering the ocean while flames clung to her legs.

The flames were an illusion, though. Gibson knew she had protected her flesh, and the fire only burned the fumes of the chemicals. There was heat, yes, but no scorching. Escaping the straitjacket while in the water was impressive, though. Gibson had never wanted to do something like that too much, though he'd done some of it in his early career. Escapology was too much physical labor. He preferred illusions, making an audience think they knew what they were seeing.

That was what made him great. That perception that others had of him.

The room was a trophy chamber of his successes. Framed pictures of performances and his meetings with celebrities filled the walls. This was his world now, not his father's. He had gone much further than his father had ever believed he would in his career, and Gibson reveled in that knowledge, even though his father would never acknowledge his success. Knowing that there was so much of it to ignore made that success even sweeter.

At the computer, he brought up the closed circuit television system he had hidden throughout the house. He watched as the woman entered the villa on Roylston's heels.

Gibson stood in the dark and awaited his

call to tonight's performance. The hunger coiled and uncoiled inside him.

Desperate, Heath threw himself from his car and went around to the trunk. He wore the .357 on his hip in a holster, but he'd stored the 9mm he'd captured from the woman in his hotel room in the trunk. Since then, he'd also gotten extra magazines and a shoulder holster from the kid who had sold him the revolver.

In the shadows under a palm tree, Heath strapped the 9 mm under his left arm, then pulled a black windbreaker on to hide the weapons. He shoved the extra magazines into the thigh pockets of his cargo jeans, then pulled on a black ball cap to cover his hair.

After closing the trunk, he jogged down to the beach and ran along the dark water. Trying to approach the villa across the light-colored sand of the beach would have made him stand out. Since the moon wasn't up, the ocean was inky dark, and he knew he was nearly invisible against it. He jogged, his feet sinking into the wet sand with liquid crunching noises.

With someone in their midst, Heath felt certain that the villa's flesh and blood security would draw closer to the core, leaving it to the electronic surveillance to watch the perimeter. Those systems weren't fail proof. During the days he had scouted the villa, Heath had felt certain there were weak points. Trespassing would have made any evidence he'd obtained that way illegal, though. So he'd kept his distance.

Tonight, all bets were off. Lauren wasn't supposed to have bearded the monster in his lair. They were supposed to have coaxed Gibson out.

He ran, his muscles warming up against the chill coming in from the sea.

The house had seemed large and ornate from outside, but once Lauren was inside, she was overwhelmed by the opulence. Chandeliers, art, plush furniture, woods, marble and window treatments that looked as though they'd been ripped from designer catalogues filled the rooms she saw as Roylston escorted her to the back of the house.

Lauren's fear had grown when she'd entered the villa's gates, and it was everything she could do to control it as she followed the bodyguard.

She made herself think of Megan, but that was a double-edged sword because that memory was as filled with terror as it was with resolve to see her sister's murderer caught.

She followed Roylston up to the second floor to a door. The bodyguard indicated the door. "Everything you need will be inside. Feel free to choose whatever you wish."

"Thank you." Lauren stepped through the doorway into a large room that contained a vanity and two large closets filled with women's clothing.

"Sure." Roylston pointed to an intercom on the wall. "If you need anything, just ring. When you're ready, let me know and I'll come get you."

"All right. Thank you." Lauren watched the man close the door, but she still didn't feel alone. She took a deep breath and tried to release the tension that she felt inside her.

She couldn't help wondering if this was what Megan had been treated to, as well. Then she knew that wasn't the case. No matter what had happened between Gibson and Megan, Lauren knew her sister would never have put up with something like this.

Yet, here she was, prepared to put on clothes Gibson had provided for his "guests." Curious, Lauren looked through the closets, wondering what kind of clothing Gibson had chosen, and wondering, too, at the women whom he brought back to the villa. During the time she and Heath had watched the villa, no one had brought a woman onto the premises.

Growing up in foster care, Lauren had endured her share of hand-me-downs, but this was a more exotic collection than she'd ever seen. The clothing wasn't all "play" wear either, though there was an assortment of that, too: catsuits and wispy lingerie. But there was also a choice of casual clothing, beachwear and cocktail dresses. There was even a range of sizes and lengths.

Lauren picked a pair of snug-fitting skinny-legged jeans and a close-fitting pullover because that outfit provided the least amount of loose material that could be used against her if she had to fight for her life. She didn't think that would be the case. Too many people knew that

Gibson had bailed her out of jail. He wouldn't dare hurt her, would he?

She took the clothing to the bathroom in the rear of the room.

Sipping from a snifter of brandy to hold the darkness in him in thrall for a while longer, Gibson watched the woman strip in the bathroom. Her body—her shape and her form and her nudity—wasn't what excited him. It wasn't even the vision of what he would do to it. What fascinated him most was the knowledge that he was about to have more power over her than anyone had ever had before.

Onscreen, the woman stepped into the shower but the heated water had fogged the windows to the point that she seemed like an illusion on the other side of the translucent glass.

He hummed in anticipation, knowing it wouldn't be much longer now. She was going to pay for upstaging him.

Chapter 21

Plastered up against the seaward wall of the villa and drenched in the darkness, Heath felt his phone vibrate in his pocket. He slid it free, thinking that Lauren might be calling him from inside the house.

Instead, Jackson Portman's face showed on the view screen.

Heath debated answering the phone, but this late in the evening with everything going on, he knew that his partner wouldn't call unless there was serious need.

"Yeah?"

"I think I know who Gibson is."

The information surprised Heath, but not the fact that Jackson had stayed with the search. "How?"

"I kept backtracking Sisco's employment to a place called Blackheart Solutions. Heard of it?"

"No."

"Don't feel bad. Neither had I until I dug in. Turns out Blackheart Solutions is a company that specializes in computer software. They get a large part of government contracts every year. Providing encryption and stuff like that."

Heath gazed up at the tall perimeter wall. "I got a thing here, Jackson. Maybe you could pick up the pace a little."

"Blackheart Solutions is owned by a man named Julius Bleak. Guy knows congressmen and presidents by their first names. He also has a son, Terrence, who is forty-three years of age. Terrence has a history of violence against women. Two charges of rape and aggravated assault in Seattle. Both cases were dismissed with prejudice because Terrence Bleak's daddy used his leverage to get the charges dropped. I had to really look for that information to get it. Terrence was nineteen and twenty-two at the time. Then Terrence vanished. No history. A few years later, Gibson starts hitting the magic circuit. How do you like that?"

"Less and less by the minute, buddy." The anxiety inside Heath reached shattering levels. All he could think about was Janet and how he hadn't been there for her. "I've got to go. I appreciate everything that you've done."

"Let me know how everything works out?"

"Definitely." Heath couldn't tell Jackson his situation. His partner would have tried to talk him down, and Heath didn't have the time for an argument. He hung up, then looked up Inspector Myton's phone number and placed a call to him.

Myton was slow to pick up, and when he did he sounded half-asleep. "Hello?"

"This is Heath Sawyer."

That perked Myton up immediately. "Where are you, Detective Sawyer? I have some questions I'd like you to answer. It seems your hotel room was trashed, and there was a shootout in front of the building that has me puzzled."

"I'm at Gibson's estate."

"Really? What are you doing there?"

"I'm saving my friend. You need to hurry." Heath hung up, turned to the security wall and walked to where the ocean lapped at the perimeter. Over the years of constant assault, the salt water had chipped away at the mortar holding the stones together, leaving hand and foot holds. He started climbing, hauling himself up as quickly as he could.

Lauren followed Roylston back down to the first floor, then to a library much like the one at Agony House, though designed on a less ambitious scale. The shelves held books and DVDs on magic, and glass display cases held dioramas of famous magicians performing legendary tricks and escapes.

Fascinated, she stopped in front of a display case that held a scene of Houdini talking to a gypsy woman seated at a table with a crystal ball. The magician had hold of the table and was yelling at the woman, who was terrified.

"Houdini didn't believe in the spirit world." Gibson had come into the room behind her without her knowledge.

"That's right." A chill passed through Lauren, but she suppressed it. She couldn't help thinking that she was looking at her sister's murderer, and that she was standing more or less helpless inside his house.

"Would it surprise you to know that I first got involved in magic because I wanted to speak to my mother?"

"I've never read that anywhere."

"I've never told anyone." Gibson gazed at the diorama. "My mother died when I was very young. I've missed her my whole life."

"I'm sorry to hear that."

Gibson shrugged and smiled. "She chose to leave. Committed suicide." He shrugged again. "At least, that's what my father tells me. He's a very powerful and influential man, so that must be true, don't you think?"

"I wouldn't know."

With slow, deliberate steps, Gibson crossed the room to gaze intently at the diorama. "Who are you, Mistress Tereza—or should I call you Lauren Cooper, since you were booked under that name—that you would come into my world and seek so strongly to attract my attention? I feel that I should know you."

Lauren was surprised to discover that Gibson still hadn't recognized her from the encounter in the restaurant days ago. "I'm a struggling magician trying to make a name for myself."

"And you choose to do this by confronting me on my turf?"

"I didn't mean any harm."

Gibson looked at her then. "Not even when you stole the show from under me at the Agony House?"

"I didn't expect you to be so confrontational. I was going to use someone else in the audience to finish the trick, but when you stepped in so hard, it had to be you."

Shrugging, Gibson lifted a hand, and a gold coin danced across his knuckles like a leaf flowing down a river, smooth and effortless. The deep yellow color of the metal winked in the light. "I couldn't let you just steal the show like that. Then, I couldn't stop you."

"I thought maybe we could work together."

"If you know anything at all about me, you know I don't work with a partner."

"I wasn't trying to be a partner. Just a warm-up act."

"And the death-defying leap from the ship into the ocean while in a straitjacket today?"

"That was to get your attention."

"Was it? Because I think it was to capitalize

on the success of the video currently going viral across the internet." Gibson smiled, and there was no humor. Malice gleamed in his dark eyes.

"A little publicity never hurts."

"This publicity? It's going to hurt you." With his other hand, Gibson snapped a card into the air.

The card whirled like a Frisbee as it crossed the distance to Lauren. Without thinking, she plucked the card out of the air.

"Very good reflexes." Gibson seemed genuinely amused.

Lauren turned the card over and saw the white rabbit there.

"After the police find your body, I'm going to mail them that card." As he strode toward her, Gibson's hands came from behind his back. In one of his hands, he held a long knife.

Heath clambered over the security wall without setting off an alarm, then dropped to the ground and ran toward the main house while staying in the shadows. The sweet, heavy scent of the bougainvillea filled his nose and almost made him sneeze.

One of the security guards emerged from the house and went to the car parked in the circular drive. The engine started with a smooth growl. The guy rested behind the steering wheel with the dome light off, the instrument panel glowing in his face. Another guard stood at the door to the house and talked on his cell phone.

Stealthily, knowing there was no turning back at this point but feeling certain that Lauren's life was in danger, Heath crept up on the man. Just behind the door, he whispered only loud enough for the driver to hear. "Move and I will kill you."

The man slowly started to raise his hands.

"Put your hands on the steering wheel. Let's not invite your friend before we need to."

After a brief hesitation, the man grasped the steering wheel.

"Is the woman still inside the house?"

"Yes."

"Is she still all right?"

"She was. She's with Gibson in the library."

A sharp feeling of relief flooded Heath.

"Doesn't mean she's going to stay that way, though. Gibson's been in the mood to kill her since she showed up at that house. You're the cop, right?"

"Yeah."

The guy pressed a hand on the horn as he shoved out of the car and rounded on Heath, catching him off guard. His hand slammed into Heath's chest because Heath didn't want to fire immediately. Thrown off-balance, Heath staggered back and watched the man bring up a pistol.

Heath squeezed the .357's trigger and felt the pistol buck as a bullet whipped past his ear. His round caught the man in the chest, and he followed it with a second round that cored through the man and shattered the door window behind him.

The man at the door brought up his pistol and took a defensive position inside the house.

Keeping a lid on the panic that filled him, not wanting to think that he was going to lose the woman he was almost certain he was in love with, Heath yanked the falling dead man out of his way and slid behind the steering wheel. Shots blasted through the windshield and tore into the passenger seat as he pulled on the safety harness. He slammed the transmission into Drive and pressed his foot down on the accelerator.

The high-performance engine thrust the car forward. Heath laid the .357 in the passenger seat and steered with both hands to bring the car on a direct path with the front of the house. He hoped the front end stayed together long enough to get him where he was going. Otherwise he was a dead man and Lauren was going to brutally die.

The front tires jerked and juddered as the car raced up the wide steps, but they navigated the incline with less trouble than he'd anticipated. The whole vehicle shook and shimmied, but he managed to hold it on course with one hand while he picked up the revolver with the other.

When the car hit the front of the house, the airbags deployed. Even though he'd prepared for the impact, even though the seat belt clamped like a vise around his chest, the face plant against the airbag rushing up at him robbed Heath of his senses.

Chapter 22

Savage joy filled Gibson when he saw the fear in the woman's eyes. That look, that palpable feel of the connection to his audience during the final performance he would give them, was an elixir that never failed to transport him out of the ordinary world. Drawn by that fear, he closed on her, eager to open her up and let the blood hit the ground.

It would be the first time he had killed in the library in front of so many of his childhood heroes. He didn't know why he hadn't done so before. No one could stop him. Nothing could get in his way. He was invincible.

The woman, Mistress Tereza, cowered before him, giving ground as he backed her toward the fireplace. She reached out and toppled a diorama of Doug Henning's performance in *Spellbound.* The display smashed across the wooden floor in front of Gibson. He snarled inarticulate curses at her. The diorama could be replaced, but he hated the idea that anyone could touch his things.

He lifted the knife and strode toward her with greater speed.

Then Roylston's mocking voice halted him. "Hey, Terrence."

In disbelief, stunned to have heard *that* name here in this house, Gibson turned toward his bodyguard. *"What* did you call me?"

Twenty feet away, Roylston stood framed by the door. He held something in his left hand and a pistol in his right. He flicked his left hand forward, and a cylindrical shape flew through the air to land at Gibson's feet.

It was a cigar.

Gibson glared at Roylston. "What is the meaning of this?"

Roylston smirked at him. "Your old man just called me. He's having another son. He doesn't need you anymore to carry on the family name." He raised the pistol to fire.

Panicked, filled with fear for himself for the first time in years, Gibson flung the knife he held. It flickered through the air like quicksilver and caught Roylston in the neck.

With a look of shock, the big man clamped a hand to his neck and pulled it away covered with blood. The pistol fell from his nerveless fingers.

Cursing, knowing that Roylston wouldn't be acting alone, Gibson raced over to pick up the pistol. He gripped it and turned around, determined to get out of the house. But first, he was going to take care of the woman. He started to turn back around, but something that sounded very much like a bomb went off at the front of the house. Security alarms screamed to life throughout the villa.

Grimly, Heath clawed back up from the thready darkness that was trying to suck him down. He forced his head up and lifted the revolver at the same time.

The man who had been hiding behind the door rose up like a ghost from the grave, covered in plaster and mortar dust that pushed into the house in a large, roiling cloud. He fired at the car, his hand suddenly filled with a muzzle flash.

Taking deliberate aim, Heath put two rounds into center body mass, following through on muscle memory he'd gotten while in the military and from hours spent on the shooting range.

The bodyguard stumbled back and fell.

Looking around, his head feeling as if it was about to shatter from all the security alarms, Heath realized the car had gotten wedged in the suddenly enlarged doorway. The doors were stuck, and he couldn't open them.

He tried to free himself from the seat belt that felt as if it was crushing the life out of him, but something had to have been broken in the locking mechanism during the crash. He had to fish out his pocketknife and cut himself free.

Breathing hurt. Moving hurt. But Heath leaned back in the seat and kicked the windshield out of the car, then turned around and crawled out after it. He almost fell when he stepped off the front of the car, but he retained his balance and flipped the revolver open, ejecting the four spent shells and replacing them with fresh rounds. He snapped the cylinder closed with a flick of his wrist and moved on into the house. He didn't know where Lauren was, but the need to find her consumed him.

He started moving toward the stairs, then heard a shot from the right. "Lauren!"

The only thing that held the fear at bay inside Lauren was the knowledge that her sister's murderer stood in front of her. Incredulous, she'd watched Gibson throw the knife with deadly accuracy, but by that time her fingers were already closing around the fireplace poker.

When Gibson went after the fallen bodyguard's pistol, Lauren had gone after him. She ignored the reluctance she felt for what she was about to do and instead stoked her rage over losing her sister. Her hands curled around the poker.

Gibson lifted the pistol and turned around, and Lauren swung the poker off her shoulder in the flat arc that her adoptive father had spent time teaching her for softball. The poker caught Gibson alongside his jaw, and bone cracked loud enough to hear in between the frantic bleats of the security alarms.

Stumbling to the side, Gibson tried to bring up

the pistol again. Stepping forward as though she was meeting a fastball pitch, Lauren swung once more, only catching Gibson on the arm that he instinctively raised to defend himself. The blow drove him to the side and down to the ground.

Lauren moved toward him and raised the poker over her head, intending to bring her weapon down on Gibson's skull. He looked up at her, his face streaming blood. All she had to do was swing and he would go away forever. She knew that.

But she also knew that wouldn't bring Megan back. Nothing would bring Megan back.

Screaming in frustration, Lauren crashed the poker through the diorama of Houdini exposing the fake spiritualist.

"You should have killed him. You know you wanted to. At least you would have had that."

Drawn by the wheezing voice, Lauren turned around to discover Roylston once more on his feet. The knife was still in his neck. He hadn't re-moved it. And he had another pistol in his hand. He waved the weapon at Gibson. "Go ahead. Bust him up like a piñata. If I do it, it won't mean as much to me. Just the end of a long, tiring job. But you? You'll get something out of it. He tried to kill you."

"He killed my sister. He killed Megan."

Frantically, Gibson shook his head in agony. Blood dripped to the floor. He pointed at Roylston.

"Megan Taylor? The woman drowned down here?"

"Yes."

Roylston chuckled despite the pain he was in. "No. That was me. This idiot tried to kill her that night, but she fought him off and got away. It was just one more case of me having to clean up his mess. Then he sent that White Rabbit card to the police. Claiming his kill. Feeding his vanity." He swallowed with effort and chuckled again. "That's funny. You coming down here, taking him on—bringing him to this, really, and it was for something that he couldn't even do right."

Gibson tried to get to his feet.

"No, you just stay where you are, you sick psychopath. I'm going to let Mistress Tereza have one more—"

Gunfire erupted somewhere in the house.

Roylston glanced back over his shoulder. Seizing her chance, with her sister's killer once more in front of her, Lauren raised the poker and raced at the bodyguard. Some sixth sense must have warned him of her approach, though, because she knew he didn't hear her. When she swung, he turned around and caught the poker in his left hand as he lifted the pistol to point at her face.

Heath zeroed in on the sound of the gunshot and came up on Roylston from behind. Over his shoulder, Heath spotted Lauren standing in front of the man, almost dwarfed by his bulk. Roylston was still holding on to the poker that Lauren had obviously swung.

Another gunshot boomed inside the room, and this time Roylston staggered back and sat down on the floor. Then he fell backward, and the thousand yard stare in his eyes revealed that he was dead.

Lauren turned, still not seeing Heath, and looked back into the room. There, kneeling on the floor, Gibson struggled to get to his feet. His jaw hung strangely, but he pointed a pistol at Lauren, and his intentions were clear.

Unable to get Lauren clear of the situation,

Heath stepped into the library with both hands on the .357. "Drop the weapon, Gibson." Heath didn't want to risk the man accidentally discharging his weapon by shooting him. "Only chance you're going to get. Otherwise I make you disappear."

Gibson blinked to focus on Heath, then nodded and slowly lowered the pistol, leaving it on the floor and lacing his fingers behind his head.

Heath reached down and untied Roylston's bloody tie, surprised to find the knife lodged in the side of his neck, then used it to tie Gibson's hands behind his back. He glanced up at Lauren, who looked as if she was ready to fall down.

"You okay? You hurt?"

She shook her head. "No. I'm fine." Studying him with concern, she crossed over to him and touched his face. "You're bleeding."

"I'm okay."

"You don't look okay."

"It's been a long day." Holding the pistol to the back of Gibson's head, his knee still firmly planted in his quarry's back, Heath reached out his free arm and held Lauren tight. "I'm really glad you're alive."

"Me, too." She leaned down and kissed his bruised lips.

Sirens screamed in the distance. Lauren pulled back.

Heath grinned. "That will be Inspector Myton. We're going to have a lot of explaining to do."

It was a *lot* of explaining. Hours passed by while Lauren sat in an interview room and talked with Inspector Myton. She had told him, then two successive investigators, an edited version of what had happened at Gibson's villa. They had agreed to leave out Sisco's kidnapping and the encounter at Heath's hotel. If the inspector wanted to pursue those events, he'd have to do it without their help.

"Well, Miss Cooper, it certainly is a most interesting—and most curious—story you and Detective Sawyer have to tell." Inspector Myton once more sat on the opposite side of the table in the interview room.

Lauren sipped her water and didn't say anything.

"I must admit, there are parts of your stories that bother me. Missing pieces, mostly." The inspector smiled. "But I am willing to let many of them go at this point. After all, the nefarious White Rabbit serial killer was brought in on my watch, was he not?"

The goodbye at the airport was hard. Lauren held on to Heath as her flight to Chicago boarded. He would be returning to Atlanta on his flight within the hour.

She'd never felt a person who completed her more than Heath Sawyer outside of her family. She didn't want to let go of that feeling. But the murders of Megan and Janet had been the only things holding them together. Freed from the shadow of the White Rabbit Killer, both of them could go back to their very separate lives.

Lauren forced herself to be neutral, to not think about the end of everything and to concentrate on the good they had done. As Heath had said, there was no telling how many lives they had saved. She cleared her throat to speak. "So how much trouble are you going to be in back in Atlanta?"

Heath shook his head. "I went way over the line. I don't know. The captain doesn't like problems, and Gibson's testimony about his father's security people are going to bring his father down, too. That guy's in tight with several government agencies." He frowned. "It's going to end up being a big deal. That's not my fault, but the captain's gonna blame me for it to a degree. It's how he is." He looked at her. "What about you? Are you going to be okay?"

"Yes." Lauren took a breath. "It's not going to be the same without Megan, but Mom and I will get through it. We got through losing Dad, too. You just don't forget, you know?"

"I know."

The airline representative made the last call for the flight to Chicago.

Lauren reached down for her carry-on. "I've got to go."

Heath nodded. "Have a safe flight, Lauren." He stepped forward and kissed her lightly on the lips. She wanted to hold on to him, but she couldn't and she knew it. Giving in to that weakness here would be hard because she knew she had to get back to take care of her mother.

And Heath had his own life.

He let her go, and she turned around and

walked toward the entrance to the boarding tunnel. She didn't look back because she didn't want him to see the tears in her eyes. Leaving was hard enough without both of them being miserable.

Epilogue

"Ladies and gentlemen, late from her last showing in Kingston, Jamaica, may I present the lovely and mysterious Mistress Tereza!" Warren Morganstern's announcer's voice was strong and loud, carrying over the PA system in the small room in the magic shop.

Once Lauren had returned home, Morganstern had insisted on hosting a show for her. They had spent the past two weeks getting everything ready, and even though she'd done every trick on the slate hundreds of times and the show was primarily invitation-only to a select audience, Lauren still felt nervous.

She hadn't ever done a real show before, only bits and pieces as interludes and warm-ups for real showmen. She launched into the table magic first, doing old tricks with occasional little personal flares that brought oohs and ahhs from the audience.

Her mother had a front-row seat and looked better than she had looked in months. The doctors had said she was in full remission. Her mom told her that she believed Megan had reached back and taken the cancer from her as a final gift.

Lauren didn't know what to believe, but she was glad to have her mom healthy.

One of the finales of the act was the disappearing cabinet. It was an old trick, too, but she'd always enjoyed it.

"Ladies and gentlemen." Morganstern was really laying it on as stage hands brought the seven-foot tall cabinet onto the stage. "As you can see, this is a simple box. A plain wooden construction of humble origins. But Mistress Tereza is going to make magical history here tonight for your viewing pleasure as she disappears from this very box."

A drumroll sounded as the box came to a stop in center stage, and that surprised Lauren because they'd never discussed that. Still, clad in her black outfit, she walked to the box and bowed, then she opened the door to show the audience that it was empty.

Only it wasn't.

Heath stood inside dressed in a tuxedo and top hat, and looking more handsome than she'd ever seen him. He winked at her, then stepped from the box toward her holding a magic wand. She stood there, not knowing what to do.

Then, with a flourish, Heath waved the wand and it turned into a bouquet of flowers. He took her into his arms and kissed her long and hard, and the sizzle of their magic spun through her body. When he drew back, she was breathless.

The crowd hooted and hollered, and from their reactions, Lauren knew Morganstern had roped them all in on the trick. Even her mother, who was clapping in delight.

"I wanted to let you know that I had a little magic of my own." Heath grinned down at her.

She smiled back. "You always have, mister."

"What would you say if I told you Chicago's finest is looking for a detective?"

Lauren repressed a smile with real effort. "Atlanta is willing to let you go?"

"It's not up to them, and they don't have the same benefits package as this city."

"Chicago's always been one of my favorites."

"We'll have to talk then. Until then, I hear you're going to disappear in this box." With theatrical aplomb that was only a little awkward but endearingly so, Heath waved to the waiting box.

"I am. But only for a little while." Lauren stepped into the box and started to close the door, then she opened it, reached back for Heath and pulled him inside with her. "I'm not letting you out of my sight tonight."

The audience rolled with laughter, evidently hearing everything over the PA pickup.

Heath held her tightly. "I've never really disappeared before."

"It's easy. I'll teach you how." Lauren leaned in and kissed him, then closed the door.

And they disappeared.

* * * * *